DEAR OPL

Shelley Sackier

sourcebooks
jabberwocky

To Chloe and Gabe,

who for years told me that I didn't have to try so hard

with my cooking.

I forgive you.

And you're welcome.

Copyright © 2015 by Shelley Sackier
Cover and internal design © 2015 by Sourcebooks, Inc.
Cover design and illustrations by Jeanine Henderson
Cover images © Lana Langlois/Thinkstock; fotyma/Thinkstock

Published by Sourcebooks Jabberwocky, an imprint of Sourcebooks, Inc.
P.O. Box 4410, Naperville, Illinois 60567-4410
(630) 961-3900
Fax: (630) 961-2168
www.sourcebooks.com

Library of Congress Cataloging-in-Publication Data is on file with the publisher.

Source of Production: Versa Press, East Peoria, Illinois, USA
Date of Production: June 2015
Run Number: 5004259

Printed and bound in the United States of America.

VP 10 9 8 7 6 5 4 3 2 1

Chapter 1

The dark enveloped me, squishing my lungs. Like the engulfing bear hug you get from an uncle who's built like a lumberjack. But this black was so tarry and thick, it made me feel as if I were breathing syrup and forced my heart to thud in my chest. I blinked again and again, and squinted hard, hoping something—*anything*—would come into focus. I wanted to sprint for my bed, to hide beneath my quilt, where nothing but fuzzy warmth and an old licorice stick are allowed. But I needed this. I couldn't leave because I had to get rid of the awful ache that poked at my sleep. If I fed it, like a lion at the zoo, it would circle and grow quiet. Sometimes.

Even though I wasn't supposed to.

My hands fluttered in front of me, like a couple of blind butterflies. They bumped against a pointed edge. I jerked back, thinking I'd been bit, but I took a breath and crept forward until I touched it once more. I traced my skittish fingers along its form until I felt certain the thing wouldn't strike at me with sharpened fangs and light up with red demonic eyes. It was a box of cereal. And it had to be Froot Loops because the pantry was a bundle of lip-smacking scents like tangy lemon, zingy orange, electric lime, and mouth-watering cherry. This meant Ollie had left the bag open and steam would shoot out of Mom's ears because it'll have gone stale by morning. I sighed with relief because as far as I knew, no one has ever been seriously injured by sugary, ring-shaped cereal. Then, again, maybe my younger brother would be the first.

I pushed the box aside and moved my hands higher up. I knocked another smaller carton to the floor, where it bounced off my sock-covered foot. I squatted, sweeping my hands across the floorboards until I found it. Bringing the package to my nose, I sniffed its edges. It smelled like Thanksgiving—well, not the last one, but the twelve others before that. It smelled of cinnamon and apples. It smelled of happiness.

I opened the box and felt inside, my fingers searching for more of the memory. They picked up a tiny pouch. A tea bag. It made the sound of Mom's old flower seed envelopes, the ones she held up each spring and shook like tiny maracas. "April showers bring May flowers! Let's go plant some future sunshine."

That didn't happen this spring. Or the one before it.

I fumbled about until I found an empty spot I could push the tea bags into and then let my fingers wander farther across the shelf. They collided into something crinkly. *Bingo!*

I pressed my hands around the package. It had the right sound—like crunching plastic—when I squeezed it. I pulled it to my nose. Yes, definitely the right smell. And not one I could attach to any other thing. It was powdery sweet. Buttery. Not quite chocolate but deep, like cocoa. It mixed with scents of sugared vanilla—a cream so luscious, it ran slickly against your tongue. This was not just a food; it was a feeling. I wanted those Oreos so badly my mouth started watering like a mini sprinkler.

I felt around for the opening, the plastic pullback tab that granted you access right to the very heart of the package and the cure-all cookies. Tonight's remedy. But something was wrong. The pull tab was missing. I groped the front and back, skimming its sides, trying to catch the sticky edge like you do when your Scotch tape has come off the metal ridge and sealed itself back onto the roll. It wasn't there. I couldn't find it.

Something brushed against my cheek and I reeled back in fright, bumping into the rickety pantry steps behind me. My fingers slapped at my face, but found only my hair falling out of its messy ponytail. With a racing heartbeat, I ventured a hand along the wall, searching for the light switch. Then I pulled back. I'd better not turn on the pantry bulb, because the glow would creep down the hall and shine like a headlight through Mom's open bedroom door. She was a super light sleeper. She could leap out of bed at the sound of a cricket passing gas on the back porch.

But I needed those cookies.

A flashlight! That's the answer. I bent down to hunt the lower shelf beneath the microwave. In my mind I could see four of them on the ledge, lined up like eager soldiers: sentries of the dark. But I bumped into one and they tumbled like dominos. I held my breath, trying to absorb the clunking sounds. I made that lungful stay put and listened, wishing I had a third ear. At the relief of no footsteps rushing into the kitchen, I grasped one of the tipsy warriors against the dark, flipped its switch, and looked at the package in my other hand. I held the Oreos all right, but they'd been double packaged, slipped inside a Ziploc bag along with a folded piece of stationery.

I sat down on the old wine crate Mom used as a step, forgetting about how badly it creaked, and unzipped the plastic bag. I pulled out the note and tilted the beam toward the words. It said:

Dear Opal,

Please don't eat these. Remember your diet.

I love you,

Mom

Chapter 2

An opal is a mineral. Not many folks know what color they are. Even opals are confused over that. They're basically colorless. It's all the impurities inside them—the gunk—that makes them whatever color they end up.

An opal isn't as ugly as a chunk of coal, which some people say is a mineral, but isn't really. You'd get that wrong on a science test. But it isn't as impressive as a diamond either. It can't compete in that world. Diamond advertisements scream, *You are loved!* If you get an opal as a present its message is sort of, *Will this do?*

My name is Opal, but I don't spell it that way. It now looks like this: OPL. I kicked out the A. I figure if Mom wants me to lose weight, maybe she'd perk up if at least my name shrunk by twenty-five percent. And even though opals come in every color of the rainbow, the regular ones, just like the inside of an Oreo, are flat and doughy. They're called *potch*. If I had to compare myself to any opal, I wouldn't be the rare, fiery red ones or the super expensive black ones. I'd be potch. Chalky white and kind of pasty. And with a lot of gunk inside. I've grown into my name. But I didn't need the cruel reminder every time I put it at the top of a spelling test.

I guess I'm lucky it's not something like feldspar or zircon or crapolite. Okay, that last one I made up, except it's pretty close. That one describes more how I feel. At thirteen, there are a lot of things that suck about being me, but the biggest thing is the thing that's making me big.

Food.

I'm food fighting. And not in the fun way. I'm not lobbing spoonfuls of mashed potatoes across the cafeteria. My battles are more with myself. Okay, and maybe Mom. Yeah, if I could hurl the mashed up mush at anybody, I'd aim at her. All she sees when she looks at me is food anyway. I'm a giant lollipop she wants to draw a red circle around and put a jagged slash through. Banned. Unwanted. Yucky.

"I've been thinking, Opal. Why don't you start a blog?" Mom said in her *I am really trying to be positive* happy voice the morning after my midnight cookie raid. "Maybe to keep an inventory of what you're eating. It could be a Bread and Butter blog." She poured coffee into a thermos, taking her time, a tiny stream from the pot to the cup.

Right beside her thermos was the Oreo bag, on display for the whole world to see. She refused to look me in the eye, and her suggestion of the blog must have been my pantry punishment. "I think it'll be easier if you kept track of things, like you do with your mittens or homework."

"Or how long it takes you to pour a cup of coffee, and how many times we get to talk about food," I mumbled so she wouldn't hear. But I wanted her to hear. Especially how much I wanted to *stop talking about food.*

"You can write about anything you want, as long as it helps you stick to your promise," Mom said, finally screwing on the thermos cap and then grabbing an armload of crumpled, messy papers before dashing out the front door with a careless wave. Dashing off to a place where everything is easier. Where work comes first and family troubles get buried. If I got to work in a library, I'd probably find it super easy to ditch my difficulties too. I bet she just reads all day about other people's happy times. I know I would.

I plopped two "against the rules" Pop-Tarts into the toaster and pushed the lever down hard. I leaned over to watch the coils blaze and turn bright orange. Waves of heat reached my face. Maybe it could melt away my fat, like butter in a skillet.

I heard G-pa's slippers swish along the kitchen floor and stop at the electric tea kettle. Neither of us said anything because we're not exactly morning people, but after my pastries popped up, I stopped at the counter where his mug of tea steeped.

G-pa came to live here after Dad left us. He set up his station in the corner of the living room. All he needed was a big stuffed armchair, an ottoman roomy enough for his feet and for me to perch on, and a little side table for his stinky tea.

"What are you drinking today?" I asked him.

"Japanese tea," he said, his voice still crusty from sleep.

"What's in it?" I looked down at the mug.

"Smell it."

I did and felt my nose shrivel up inside itself. "Ick. It smells like twigs."

"Then your nose is off," he said after a sip. "It's roasted twigs."

I pinched my nose and eyes together, squeezing everything into one space. He'd think I was making a face about his tea, but I was actually trying to keep from cracking up. I didn't want G-pa to know I thought he was funny. Because then he might stop trying to make me laugh. It was our contest. And I wasn't ready for it to be over.

I moved away to the kitchen table and put my Pop-Tarts next to my open laptop. I tucked my earbuds in and tapped on my favorite morning playlist. Then I thought about Mom's last words. *You can write about anything you want, as long as it helps you stick to your promise.*

But Mom had said the same thing when she gave me the journal with the purple, wavy psychedelic cover. And the old electric typewriter that punched a hole in the paper anytime I used the letter Y. It was as if that key was super hyper and on a Red Bull diet. Or maybe it only wanted me to pay attention to the words *candy* or *Dairy Queen* or *mayonnaise*.

When journaling didn't take, Mom had plastered the refrigerator door with before and after pictures of skinny women in swimsuits.

She had said, "It's hard for a person to commit to change, Opal, but if you feel like you aren't alone in the battle, it lightens the load."

I had studied the pictures with a magnifying glass. Those women weren't even human because our science book says we have twelve ribs. I could count all of theirs, and I never got past nine.

After Mom went to bed, I'd usually sneak downstairs in my double thick hiking socks. They have yet to go hiking, but it's like wearing pillows on your feet. No one hears you coming. Not even the pretend women on the fridge. Then I'd fill a jumbo blue mixing bowl with Frosted Flakes, muffling the sound as much as I could, sprinkle it with

Nesquik, and drench it with chocolate milk. Somehow it filled the hole. Made me less see-through. Even for just a little bit.

Finally, she bought me a laptop. "You can take it anywhere, Opal: in the car, in your room, and most importantly, in the kitchen. You can track everything you're eating. That will be an eye-opener. It can be a Junk Food Journal."

"How about a Waste of Time Diary?" I snapped. If she could come up with a new nickname for this crummy catalogue idea every day, then so could I.

"Sure," she had said, staring at the chaos on her desk. Her hand waved in the air toward me, as if she were reaching for something in the dark. "Whatever will keep you on the right track."

The *right track*, according to Mom, will finally allow her to buy me a pair of skinny jeans. I don't want skinny jeans. I want sweat pants. Jeans are so uncomfortable with the rough fabric, the tight waistband, and no room to balloon when my stomach bloats. Once I zip them up, whatever can't fit inside pops out and rests on top, spilling over like cake batter in a bowl too small.

What really bothers me is that if I do as Mom wants—if I manage to finally get myself into a pair of skinny jeans—I'd disappear in front of her. No more Opl. Trouble fixed.

I'm a problem not a person. But Dad was a problem she couldn't fix, and he disappeared from our lives too. It feels like we're all on our way to disappearing in front of Mom. Maybe that's what she wants. *Poof.*

And why are we still wearing jeans anyway? It's an out-dated material made for California gold miners. I live in Virginia, in a town that won't let you chip away at anything because one of our dead presidents may have walked on it or leaned against it. Plus, mining is not in the school's curriculum, so why should I dress like I'm nugget hunting? Unless they're McNuggets. Still, buying those pants neared the top of Mom's nonstop to-do list. But getting me into them was nearer.

I broke off a chunk of my Pop-Tart and flung it at Mr. Muttonchops, our dog. He raised his hairy head just in time to snatch it out of the air, swallow it whole, and resettle himself beneath the bridge G-pa made with his legs up on the ottoman. G-pa raised one furry, white eyebrow at me.

"He's helping me with my new diet," I said, shrugging.

G-pa went back to tapping on his tiny laptop, which he was still trying to get the hang of using. He said he figured if he wanted to talk to me or my little brother, Ollie, then he'd have better luck emailing us rather than shouting to get our attention, since we are glued to our computer screens with our earbuds in. I've told him a hundred times that he has the Caps Lock button on, but he doesn't seem too fussed. Most of what G-pa says is extra loud anyway.

G-pa and Ollie were the only people on my side. They knew how hard I struggled to pass up a second helping of dinner. According to Mom, *portion control* was my number one enemy. According to G-pa, Mom slid into second place.

SHE'S BIG INTO SETTING GOALS NOW. YOU'RE ONE OF HER PROJECTS. G-pa's email showed up on my laptop, sent from across the room. He must have heard Mom and me in the kitchen before he'd come in for his tea.

I looked up at him. He shook his head.

In fact, he must have kept his head shaking the whole day long while I was at school because at suppertime he was still doing it, only now it was over something even more ridiculous. G-pa absorbed everything that went on in our house from his chair. And spat out the stuff he thought was bunk. He thinks people talk too much, that they use fancy language to scare you into quiet. *SAY WHAT YOU MEAN. DON'T WASTE WORDS*, he'd emailed after hearing me try to tell Mom I wasn't a big fan of fat-free potato chips.

That's another of my problems. Not only did I gulp down a lot of food, but I swallowed stuff I wanted to say. Telling people what you really think is a surefire way to bring on sour faces. And ever since Dad's been gone, I've seen nearly two years' worth of faces in this family that range from salt-crusted to bitter.

TAKE A PAGE FROM OLLIE'S BOOK. HE DOESN'T GIVE A RIP WHAT PEOPLE THINK. G-pa was right. Ollie was six and wore mostly old Halloween costumes. All of them meant for girls. He'd started this habit once Dad left us. And by left us, I mean died. I just refuse to put it that way.

It was quick. And came as a big surprise. Even to Dad. One minute we were carving pumpkins on the kitchen table, and the next he got really sick and was holding my hand in his hospital bed saying, *Everything happens for a reason.*

But his doctors sure didn't have one that made sense to me.

He used to tell us that there was nothing he wouldn't eat, but suddenly there was nothing he *could* eat. He said everything the hospital made tasted bad and he wasn't hungry. Mom would bring in food, but I knew he wasn't eating it. I tried helping him—the way he used to help Ollie—by me taking a bite and then trying to get him to take one. I ended up eating Dad's bites too because it made me feel like I could help him not slip away. His cancer was a lot hungrier than he was. I'm glad that

Ollie doesn't remember much. I think we'd have a heck of a lot more than just his wearing of girls' costumes to worry about.

Tonight, Ollie came down the stairs to the dinner table dressed as either Lady Gaga, an ER nurse, or a distressed Disney maiden—it was hard to tell, but it sure made Mom's face pinch up.

"It's just a phase," she said to G-pa. "He's lacking a good male role model."

G-pa quickly emailed me, *THIS PROVES I SHOULD BELCH AND SWEAR MORE.*

I looked up from my computer and gave him one of the sour-pickle faces.

Ollie started acting super practical about my *situation* as Mom liked to call it. "I think if you're hungry, you should eat." He plucked the Pillsbury biscuit off his plate and plopped it on mine. I wanted to squish him with a hug. Instead, I glanced over my shoulder to see if Mom saw, but her eyes stayed glued to the mess on her desk. I wondered if her forbidden food radar would kick in.

It didn't.

Mom had just rented space in an old building she wanted to turn into a bookshop and was up to her earballs in work. She was always mumbling about how hard it was trying to get money from Dad's life insurance policy, and until she did, she had to keep working as many shifts at the library as they would give her.

It didn't matter. I couldn't imagine any amount of money that could help with the new bookshop. The place was a dump, boarded up for years. And our town was desperate for a bookstore since none of the big chains were allowed to mess up our dead presidents' ground. She wanted to get the shop open before Christmas, in less than four months, but it was probably way more than she could handle. This was why we never had dinner together, like they do on TV.

Mom ate at her desk, which is an old card table she bought at a garage sale and set up in the corner of the kitchen. Ollie and I ate at the kitchen table, scattered with all my homework, textbooks, and library books. And now, my laptop as well. And G-pa ate in his chair, reading his online newspaper before catching the Evening News with Gina Jacobs. *THAT'S ONE CLASSY DAME WHO DOESN'T TALK TURKEY*, he wrote after her interview with the first lady. *SHE KNOWS HOW TO GET TO THE REAL PERSON. SHE GOES RIGHT TO THE UNDERNEATH.*

I'd bet Gina Jacobs is a great mom. She doesn't talk to people about what they're wearing or how their hair looks. G-pa was right. She sees their insides.

I heard Mom crumple up the wrapper from a breakfast bar—her dinner—and watched her toss it into the garbage beneath her desk. She looked at the garbage for a few seconds and then went back to work.

"Don't forget to start that blog, Opal honey. Remember to write down all the things you eat to keep track of them." Mom waved that hand around in the air again without looking up from her papers and then tucked some of her blond hair back on top of her head with a pencil.

I wished I had hair like Mom. Not the way her hair looked now, but the way it used to be. Happy hair. Perky. Mine is the color of muddy water. Mud has a hard time being bright-eyed and bushy-tailed. I keep it in a ball, all bunched up in back, so I don't have to see any of it fall down around my shoulders. I never look at mirrors anymore. It's not that I have a huge nose or ears that stick out or even eyes that grow too close together. I have all the right features in all the regular places. Except now, I have two chins.

I dragged the laptop close to my dinner plate and noticed a new email from G-pa. *I DON'T THINK YOU NEED TO WRITE A GROCERY LIST OF FOOD AS IT DISAPPEARS DOWN YOU PIEHOLE. USE THE FORUM AS IT WAS MEANT TO BE USED. BLOG IS JUST A FANCY WORD FOR VENT. GO FOR IT.*

If I thought about it, I'd have to say that Mom sees the inside of me too. But it's only the inside of my stomach, so it hardly counts in my opinion. It never used to be that way. Before Dad died, the first thing she noticed about me every day was my smile or my eyes or the fact that it was about time for another hug. Not that I had chocolate above my top lip and *how come?*

I decided to take G-pa's advice. For the next half hour, I followed the directions my computer gave me to set up a blog. It was super easy. I don't doubt Mr. Muttonchops could have done it himself. As a reward, I tiptoed over to the pantry and pulled out a few of the Oreos. Mom was wrestling with her own computer problems, so she didn't hear the plastic crinkle beneath her stream of grumbles. One of G-pa's eyes caught both of mine, and I watched his eyebrow arch like the top half of a question mark. I looked away.

Back at my laptop, the sweet smell from the only pitch-black food I know reached my nose. I let the ridges rub against my lips. I needed to think of a good name for my blog. It had to sum up everything.

"Oh, Opal," Mom said, slumping into the chair across from me. She looked at the Oreos with bleak, puffy eyes, the same way she looks at the endless line of black ants that march into the kitchen every summer. She clucked her tongue and sunk onto the table.

I thought about the *Dear Opal, you're fat* letter from last night. It's not the first one I've gotten. I'm pretty sure she has a drawer full of stationery, all waiting patiently for their turn, all with the crisp, black headline *Dear Opal* printed at the top.

"This is too hard." Mom's arms wrapped around her head and muffled her voice. I heard her forehead clunk against the wood. She looked up just above her forearms to frown at me. "You shouldn't be eating those. Those are not the diet cookies I bought for you. Didn't you see those in the pantry?"

Saw them and ate them. I just stared at Mom.

"You know the deal, Opal. The low-fat and diet things I buy are all yours. It's your special food. Ollie and G-pa have promised not to touch it. They get just regular, old plain food."

I put the Oreo down.

"Thank you," Mom said with a weak smile. "I just want to help. I'm *trying* to help. How you look on the outside can tell people something about your insides. It's something I need to remember for the bookshop. I want people to find me…approachable. Maybe that thought can help you too."

Help me? How does *Opal you're too fat to be likeable* help?

She picked up the Oreos. "Don't look so sad, my sweet Opal." She planted a kiss on my forehead and left with my treasures. Left me…her *sweetless* Opl.

20

I wondered if she would hide them now. Or maybe put a new *Dear Opal* letter in the bag. It didn't matter. At least she gave me a blog title. And a way to prove I was a whole lot more than a file cabinet of food.

Gina Jacobs would be proud. I wasn't going to talk about turkey either. I was going to find my own underneath.

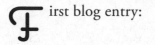

irst blog entry:

My name is Opl, I'm thirteen years old, and this is my blog. My mom wants it to be a food journal. A log of chow. But I can't see that being a good idea at all. Then it would just be a catalogue of crimes. My grandfather says I should use it to write about things that make me angry. He says it'll be more interesting than listing everything I eat. It's true. Anything would be more interesting than that. And because I know my mom will never read this, I might as well unbolt the floodgates.

Number one. No more Tylenol syrup. It's now pills. I hat sucks.

Number two. Kids who don't wash their hands after they go to the bathroom. I see it all the time and it's disgusting. Everything you touch in school has already been touched by somebody else who didn't wash their hands. It is the world's most super-gross thing. Except for seeing grown-ups kiss. That's grosser.

Number three. Getting in trouble for falling asleep in my boring history class. Pinching doesn't work. Wiggling gets me snapped at. And you can't listen to our teacher's voice. It's a soft, buzzy drone. Within thirty seconds, it feels like my brain is being sucked out of my skull. My eyes spin around to the back of my head just before my chin slides off my hand. Last week I had to walk around looking only to the left for two days because I wrenched a neck muscle.

Finally, I'd like to complain about our school's new lunch menu rule as of today. Last year my lunch was perfect. Monday through Friday at exactly 11:50, my grade went to the cafeteria. My plate held a double cheeseburger with ketchup, mustard, and extra mayo—pickle on the side. I also had cheese fries with extra cheese—except on Fridays, it was chili fries. And finally, I adored my jug of chocolate milk. I loved that lunch. I needed that lunch. And now someone has taken away the chocolate milk and replaced it with plain.

PLAIN!

I asked one of the lunch ladies if there was more in the back, but she just shook her white-netted hair at me.

"Well, where's the strawberry milk?"

She pressed her lips together.

"Did the milkman run out? Why are we short?" I wanted to bang my tray on the counter. This needed fixing. And fast.

Another woman leaned over the cash register and barked, "New state policy. No. Flavored. Milks."

"What?" I actually thought my shoulders were going to fall down to where my elbows hung. I was that disappointed. I'd been hearing the annoying buzz about some schools around us making changes like this. But not my school. My school was fine the way it was.

Tomorrow I'll bring in a container of Hershey's syrup and store it in my locker until lunchtime. "Never mind," I told the lunch ladies. "Today I'll have a blue Gatorade."

I can think of a bunch of other stuff I'm all huffy about these days, but it's getting late. I'm not sure how I feel about this bloggy thing, mostly because Mom has high hopes pinned on its big ole donkey butt. It's no different than the rest of my silly diaries. Except now my bellyaching is electronic.

Later gator,

Opl

I pressed the Publish button, sending my gripes out to the World Wide Web. The big black hole where lots of people talk, but nobody really listens. It was a little like our house but without the furniture. Okay, maybe that's not entirely true. G-pa and Ollie have big eyes and open ears, but Mom has developed a case of convenient blindness and hearing loss. G-pa and Ollie might be like a couple of comfy chairs, but it feels as if Mom had a huge garage sale and sold everything I used to like about her. It's pretty empty.

The next day at morning break, I showed Summer my new diary blog on my laptop. My best friend since she and her family moved here from England in second grade, Summer has been with me through thick and thin. Literally. She never holds anything back and gives her opinion on everything whether you asked for it or not. She told me once that I make her laugh, and since she thinks the English are the funniest people in the world, and because she misses home, I'm her substitute. Apparently, my sense of humor must be growing just as much as my body.

"I think it's a good idea to have someone be the voice for eighth graders," she said in her perfect English lilt after reading my blog post.

I looked at her sideways. "I'm not the voice of our grade." I hopped from foot to foot. I had to use the bathroom.

"Sure you are. Don't you think we're all a little nervous about choking on Tylenol tablets? And that everyone in history class wishes they had a pillow for a desktop?"

I shrugged. "I suppose." The bathroom prayed on my mind a lot lately. For some wonky reason, I had to use it all the time. It was hard to concentrate on what people were saying when you needed to pee.

"And everyone's wound up about the new milk menu. I think you speak for us all."

"Huh," I said, nodding and pulling her toward the girl's room. "Glad I could do my part." I used to have a big mouth, back before the rest of me got big, but not a big mouth large enough to cover the entire grade. Now I did a lot less chatting, mostly because I was too busy chewing. Okay, and maybe because talking meant eye contact, and I know from experience that other people's eyes rarely stayed glued to mine. They wandered to places I didn't want them staring at. Better to keep quiet and keep chewing. But maybe I would try round two of wind-bagging on my blog tonight after supper.

On my way home from school, I thought a lot about what to write. It helped to keep my mind off the fact that I had to pass the soup kitchen. Well, the soup kitchen wasn't really on my route home, but passing by it was the zippiest path to Diggerman's Mom and Pop Sweetshop and that *was* a necessary stop between my classroom and my bedroom. Actually, I've never seen a Mrs. Diggerman. Maybe she only works in the back and doesn't know how to handle customers. Or maybe Pop Diggerman thought it necessary to add a female to the sweetshop's name, because otherwise, it's just some old guy selling candy to little kids.

The red-and-white gingham awning was like a giant, colorful eyelid winking at every kid who passed by. It flapped an encrypted message, like G-pa's old Morse code machine, naming everything inside: candy bars, licorice, gum, sodas, and chips. Exactly what I needed to absorb the prickly bits of the day. Pop Diggerman liked to say he understood how times were tough for kids and he hoped to make life's bitter medicine go down a little sweeter.

Mom doesn't know about Diggerman's, and she has no idea that's where I spend every penny of my weekly allowance, but she's warned me plenty of times about the soup kitchen and to stay far away. She said the people there are rough and dangerous. So each time I've passed, I zip on by. But there's a hitch in my zip. Every day I saw the same man out front, sitting on one of the four steps up to the building's entrance. His clothes were dirty, his beard bristly, and his hair was tied back with a twist tie. He holds the same ragged Styrofoam cup and has a cardboard sign perched at his feet. It says, "Will work for food."

I hated that sign. It made me feel like I had rocks in my stomach. And this made zipping a lot harder. I closed my eyes for four steps, opened them for a quick peek at the pavement, and closed them for another four. My breath *whooshed* out in a big sigh. I'd make it to the other side of the steps and only catch a glimpse of his battered shoe.

Having gotten my afternoon stash, I made it home and found Ollie at the front door, dressed as Lady Macbeth. He wore my costume from last year's middle school play. My part was to walk around looking miserable and guilty. Sometimes I feel like I'm still playing her part.

"Hey, Opal? What would happen if you stood on your head and threw up?"

I looked at Ollie. "Why, don't you remember?"

His eyes went wide. "Did I see it happen?"

"Experienced it, you big doofus. Three years ago after

Thanksgiving dinner. You bounced around way too much and then hung upside down on your swing set with cousin Pearl."

"Cool," he said with a face-splitting grin.

"Eww. Not cool, Ollie. Icky. Very icky."

He licked his lips. "I think I remember now." He sprinted up the stairs to his room and I threw my backpack onto the kitchen table. G-pa snoozed in his chair, his late-afternoon nap in full swing, but I didn't have to tiptoe around. He said if you can't sleep through a little noise, you weren't tired enough to begin with.

I walked into the pantry—my favorite room in the house—and scanned the shelves for something to ditch Ollie's awful memory dredging. Chocolate usually helped. What was I saying? Chocolate *always* helped.

Mom kept all the really good stuff on the top shelf, but you needed the pantry steps to reach it, and she hadn't figured out that I've found her hiding spot. Toblerone and Ghirardelli live up there side by side, eyeing one another and competing for my attention. I told them I wasn't here to judge and grabbed some of each. You had to treat chocolate fairly and you had to eat it super quick. Otherwise it would turn on you and go all white and gross looking. Mom said it wasn't mold, just old. So I made sure our chocolate never felt neglected.

Once I'd gotten my other afterschool snack of G-pa's potato chips and the diet root beer Mom bought for me, I made a dash to my room, laptop under one arm, food under the other. That way, Mom didn't have to see me eat and G-pa's snoring wouldn't bother me.

I dumped everything on my bed and scrambled to my closet to pull out the one thing I managed to salvage of my dad's. It was a big sweatshirt. It said, *Inconsistency. It has its ups and downs.* I stripped off my tee and pulled the sweatshirt over my head. It still smelled of him. Just a little. A bit like soap, but the big green bar he'd used, not the kind I have. I had to remember to be extra careful so it won't need washing. I didn't want to lose that too.

I rolled over on my scrappy blue-and-green checkerboard quilt and looked up at the ceiling. It was September, which meant it was ladybug season. They scrunched together along the ceiling above my window, a convention of crimson-colored beetles chatting about the unusually warm weather. Dad used to stalk them with a Dustbuster. He looked so smug afterward, holding the vacuum up with one hand. The ladybugs buzzed around in a bright red panic inside the clear plastic case that had a wad of tissue stuffed in the end to keep them from escaping. "Now beware to the rest of you!" he'd shout. "Let this be a lesson! We will not harbor squatters!"

I counted the ladybugs. When finished, I pulled out my bedside drawer and the bag of M&M's inside it. "Twenty-four, twenty-five…twenty-six. That's one for each bug you're not here to take care of."

I scooped them up from my bed and popped them all in my mouth. I closed my eyes and tasted nothing but the sugar-crisp coating as the multicolored pebbles slowly dissolved. Then their flavor bloomed into the gooey thickness of melting chocolate. That's how I felt: easy to break on the outside, heavy and dark on the inside. Suddenly I had a horrible feeling like there was a giant fist squeezing my heart.

"You're supposed to be here. Why aren't you here?" My eyes went hot and a huge bubble of breath shot up from my stomach. I couldn't breathe. Couldn't get enough air. "Why aren't you here?" I panted. I squished my face into my pillow and wailed the question again, trying to push the words ahead of my panicky gasps for breath. I stopped, listening for an answer.

No one heard me. No one ever did.

I took a few more deep breaths, waiting for it to be easier. I wiped my eyes and sat up. I opened my laptop and went to a clean, white page. I needed to think about something else. Anything else. Homework or the maybe the blog. Eventually, the weight of an English assignment won out.

English 8

September 25th

My Greatest Achievement Thus Far

First of all, it's necessary to define achievement. My online dictionary, *Merriam-Webster*,
says it's one of several possibilities.

a. a result gained by effort
b. a great or heroic deed
c. the quality and quantity of a student's work

If I answer with "a" in mind, I would say
surviving PE class. There are few people who
can breeze through the President's Challenge
fitness test. I have seen many people crash and
burn during the dreadful few days when Coach
screams at us to, "Overcome your bodies by
utilizing your minds!"

Most of us shrink when someone shouts in
our ears to Move faster! or Stay up! or Get up!
And frankly, hollering, "Move your big fat butt,
toots!" when I jog past will only slow me down as

I spend precious seconds swiveling my head back and forth to see who heard. This happens right before I plow into the person in front of me, tripping us and adding extra time to our Endurance Run score as well as scrapes to our knees.

And if this isn't bad enough, the Flexed-Arm Hang should be banished as a spectator test. It should be done in private. Some of us cannot keep our bodies in the air once you pull out the chair, no matter how many promises and prayers fill the space of the gymnasium. I have heard that angry parents phoned the school because of the chipped teeth their child received when their arms gave out after five or six seconds. There is no honor in sporting the President's Badge with no teeth for the pictures.

Now, if "b" is my definition, eating my grandfather's icky Polish soup each year at Easter would fall into the category of great and heroic. This soup is called *czernina*. You pronounce it chudnina or yuckola. It contains duck blood. Yes, the blood from a duck—who might not have even been finished using it himself.

Lastly, look again at the final definition

of "achievement" from old *Merriam*. The "quality" and "quantity" of a student's work are two different things. Hugely different. Depending on who assigns the work, one is much more important than the other. Some days I can hand in three pages worth of sweat with impressive-sounding words, only to get it back the next day with the phrase, "Pure drivel" scrawled across it—although it could have been "Purple drizzle" because I found the teacher's handwriting impossible to read. Other times I'll churn out one measly paragraph and see my teacher tap-dance with glee. I don't begin to understand the faculty, but I'm guessing it has a lot to do with time-of-day grading. An under-caffeinated teacher can wreak havoc with my score.

If teachers let us in on which they prefer—quality or quantity—we wouldn't waste time guessing. Any chance you could discuss this at the next after-school faculty meeting? Answers will help us all breathe easier. If I succeed in fixing this school-wide dilemma, I would have to say it will be my greatest achievement thus far.

I reread my English assignment for spelling errors and other fluff. I had to stop the flow of writing twice because my bladder screamed in my ear about its own flow.

I decided it was good enough to hand in to Mr. Vandevart and also worthy of adding to my little blog diary. It showed a lot of complaining. I threw a quick "Over and Out" and "Opl" on the end of it and clicked Publish. Mom might leap with joy because while writing, I ate only half the can of Pringles rather than the three-quarters I would have scarfed down while reading or watching TV. Maybe this new diet would work out just fine.

Chapter 4

School the next day started off the same as ever. I'm used to walking through the hallways to my locker as some sort of ghost. Most kids never see me, which is a heck of a lot better than the ones who do. They quickly look down, hide their faces behind their hands as they whisper something to their locker buddies, or step back with showy gestures to allow me to pass. I hate morning arrival.

Kids use this time to inspect each other, to see what they're wearing and how cool or uncool it looks on them. You hear a lot of, "Oh, I remember you wore that last week," or "You have to let me borrow that!" ping-ponging across the hallways. No one ever commented on my clothes, but the up and down glances that went from my shoes to my shoulders easily said, *What a joke.*

By lunchtime I'd usually grown paranoid. Like there might be a message taped to my back or some gossip flying through the middle school. But by then I always found

Summer at our favorite picnic bench beneath the old beech tree, and she most often managed to boost me up until the bell rang for dismissal. Summer is a "fixer" and she loves to solve other people's problems. She works like human duct tape, but her job was cut out for her today, I thought, plopping down across from her.

"What a pain to have to pack our own lunches." I tipped my brown paper bag upside down, scattering the contents across the rough wooden planks. Mr. Souresik, our principal, had asked that we bring food from home. He said the cafeteria would stay open for those who needed it, but had limited supplies. They were *cleaning house*. That meant I'd had to make lunch myself, and I wasn't sure I'd packed enough chocolate to get me through math and history. After that was PE. I hoped to sprain a hand from writing too much in one of my next classes so I could get a note from the school nurse, excusing me from volleyball. Frankly, any sport with a ball should just be named dodgeball.

Summer took out her crustless cucumber and cream cheese sandwich and a thermos of Earl Grey tea. This is the scariest tea man has ever made. It tastes like you're drinking perfume. "I think you should write about it," she said, dabbing at her mouth with a cloth napkin. Summer thought paper napkins were barbaric, like using dried leaves to wipe your face.

"What do you mean?" I said with a mouthful of baloney. I found all napkins pointless since I had a sleeve.

"On your blog. Like you did last night. That bit about the duck blood soup was revolting, but the rest I found brilliant."

Now when Summer says the word *brilliant*, she doesn't mean whatever she's describing is sparkling but totally rockin'. It's the English equivalent of the American *sweet*.

"Wow. I almost forgot I showed you the blog. I probably shouldn't have—it's stupid. Don't bother reading anymore. I sort of feel…silly." I felt my Ritz Cracker sandwich lurching about in my stomach, so I gulped more chocolate milk to calm things down.

Summer peered at me across the rim of her thermos. "Opal…I already forwarded your blog on to everyone in my address book."

The calming wasn't working. "What?"

"I hadn't realized it was private. I thought you knew blogs were meant for everyone to read." Her eyes darted, looking at everything except me. "And they were both…brilliant. I always forward things on—if they're worth reading."

Cold panicky prickles crept through my arms and legs. The hair across my neck stood up. I had to use the bathroom. "Just how many people are in your address book?"

She bit her lip. "Only family and friends. Nobody else."

"Summer…how many?"

"Maybe one hundred…or two…hundred?"

My lunch thought better about staying in my stomach. It wanted out. "Two hundred?" I shouted.

She nodded, tucking her head deep between her shoulders. "They're mostly friends from England. They don't even know you. Well, maybe half are from England. Some people know you. Like our dentist, Dr. Brocksten, but that's only because he's your dentist too."

My head thunked onto the table. I missed landing on my Twinkie by an inch. It didn't matter. I'd be branded with *Idiot* across my forehead either with the Twinkie filling or without. I couldn't look at her. I just moaned into the table. "Everyone will read about my Flexed-Arm Hang. And about Coach shouting, "Move your big fat butt." What am I going to do?"

Summer reached an arm across the table. "I've not seen a thing in your blog that pinpoints who you are. There are plenty of Opals in the world. Besides, you've gotten good reviews."

I raised my head. "What do you mean reviews?"

Summer's shoulders slumped, a bleak look creeping into her eyes. It's what happens whenever she realizes just how far behind her I am. "Have you not checked out the comments section beneath your blog? The place where people get to say what they think about your writing? You know, if they like it or not?"

I grabbed two fistfuls of my hair. "Ugh! I totally forgot about that part." I shook my head in despair. "Unbelievable. It's just like school, isn't it? Only worse. Instead of handing my writing in to just one teacher, it's sent to the whole school, and everyone gets a chance to tell me what a loser I am."

She raised an eyebrow at me. "Chances are no one will recognize you. You never used your last name. And nobody said you're a loser, Opal. Well, at least not the last time I checked. You might want to take a look yourself."

"I'll be sure to do that. Right before I pick up my Nobel Prize in Stupidity."

When the bell rang for school dismissal, I dashed out the side entrance, my backpack slung lopsidedly over my shoulder and one shoelace unraveling with each hurried step. For once I intended to pass up the most important and anticipated part of my day: my refill at Diggerman's. Instead, I'd have to tap into my emergency stash. Right now, I had to get home fast. That still meant going past the soup kitchen. I needed to see if people had made any snarky comments about me yet. Maybe then I could put a stop to this bloggy business.

What had Mom been thinking when she asked me to do this? Did she know the whole world would read my gripe about being the size of a tank? I couldn't believe I was such a dork.

I felt something shift in my backpack and then heard the sound of spilling candy on the sidewalk cement. I twisted to look and stepped on my trailing shoelaces. The foot that wanted to move forward remained stubbornly attached to the shoe whose laces hid beneath my other foot. I was going down.

The part of me that landed on my backpack, which had slung to the side, was cushioned by the remaining jelly beans and a slightly crunchy science book. The part of me that landed on the sidewalk was less lucky. A scraped and bleeding knee peeked through a gaping hole in my stretchy black pants with the elastic waistband. My elbow bled too, but not quite as bad. The part most damaged was my pride. I saw it spill from my body, roll three feet from where I lay sprawled, and flop to a dead stop at the bottom of the steps in front of the soup kitchen. It rested at the feet of the greasy geezer with his food sign.

He looked down at me. My breath sucked into the bottom of my toes. I felt naked. His eyes shot straight through to all the marshmallowy parts I was usually able to hide beneath. "Are you okay? Are you well?" he asked me in an accent that spoke of hush puppies and sweet potato pie.

Oh my gosh! The food man talks! I didn't know what to say. We'd never spoken before. I got to my feet and looked at my pants. Then at him. "I've been…weller."

He nodded. "Me too."

I took off. I didn't even bother to pick up the spilled candy. I left it with the part of me still lying at the bottom of the stairs.

When I got home and up to the safety of my bedroom, I launched my backpack onto my floor and watched the remaining jelly beans scatter across the carpet, bumping into the poppy flower throw rug in front of my bed. I gave the necessary first aid to my knee and elbow, and then decided to do homework lying down next to those beautiful beans. Let's see how long they lasted.

Even though I'd planned to go straight to my bare-all blog, I discovered a slight snag: if I saw all the rude and nasty comments people wrote about me, I'd bury my head under a pound of quilts and then fill it with two pounds of chocolate. I'd never do my homework. So my curiosity would have to fester away while I did the mind-numbing math and science torture.

An hour dragged by with my eyes glued to my textbooks. But of course, I needed two bathroom breaks. Just as I pulled out my English homework, Ollie walked in, dressed as a six-year-old hooker with conically shaped boobs. Or maybe he was Madonna.

"If I stood two feet from the middle of a trampoline and a four-thousand-pound man dropped from two thousand feet, would I go flying?" he asked, his eyes wide with possibility.

"Not sure. I just finished my math homework and fried my brain. No more number problems, sorry." I scooped up the last handful of jelly beans and offered him some. Dad should be here to answer these questions. We'd counted on him. Like air. Or the sun. Or YouTube.

"What about if it was a two-pound man?"

I put my head down on the floor and let the beans slide out of my palm and back to the carpet. "I don't know, Ollie," I moaned. "I've got enough problems to work out today. Maybe you can ask G-pa?"

Ollie repositioned his drooping cones, probably party hats from somebody's birthday. "He's taking a nap."

"What I wouldn't give for one of those," I said, pulling my English notes in front of me. "Is Mom home?" I hadn't heard the front door yet, so maybe she was picking up takeout from Gassy Jack's again. Gassy Jack's had the best barbecued ribs and Kung Pao chicken anywhere. It's owned by a guy from Louisiana and his Chinese wife, Sheila. Sometimes they tried to mix their recipes. The chicken chow mein cobbler sounded worse than it tasted.

"Nope. But I bet you'll hear her when she comes in and sees me. This may be the one."

"The one what?" I looked up at him.

"The one that works."

I yawned, too tired to go on with his line of thinking and needed to do my English before I could check out the dreaded blog site. "Okay, buddy. I'm sure it might be too."

He looked hopeful and crossed his fingers at me before leaving.

Turning back to my English, I noticed Mr. Vandevart had given us another essay assignment entitled *How Do You Cure Boredom?* I rolled my eyes, cracked open my laptop, and began writing.

I have seen campaigns showing pictures of hungry children wearing nothing much apart from a hopeful look. The question following these images asks, "How do we cure hunger?" I have seen pink ribbons on cars and sweat-shirts, tie clips and windows, all asking us, "How do we cure cancer?" I have even sat through my grandfather's yearly lecture come deer and turkey hunting season and now know the answer to, "How do we cure meat?" But I haven't come across the answer to a problem that doesn't exist. At least in my world.

Define boredom. I've never experienced it before. Are there symptoms? Is it like a tickle in your throat or dribbly sniffles?

Hold on a second. Let me ask a friend. Okay, I'm back. I just texted two. Neither one of them knows what you're talking about. Oh, wait. Yes, we do. History class. If I'm right, only one cure exists: hearing the bell ring.

All kidding aside, your average kid knows almost nothing about boredom. We have more things to entertain ourselves with than most people have had hot dinners. We've got cell phones and smartphones, computers and Game Boys, Wiis and iPods. If we choose (not that any of us actually could), we wouldn't have to learn how to read because programmed voices can narrate any tale out loud to us from our e-readers. There's even a gadget that will plug in our own voice—or anyone else's we want—to read the story to us. We can create hip-hop tunes and wicked rap songs, jingles for commercials, or even an entire film score with nothing more than laptop software. Who needs piano lessons?

Plus, there are kids in my class who had to take violin lessons, play soccer, and spring around in tutus for ballet classes long before first grade. I don't think many of us had a chance to learn to color. There wasn't time.

Then there's the problem of school. I think teachers believe kids have twenty-seven-hour days, and they've put us to a challenge, betting on just how much homework it will take to break the camel's back.

So the question of how to cure boredom is super confusing. No offense, but I'd love to see just how many of us get the opportunity to experience the bliss of boredom. And remember, history class does NOT count.

I sat back and looked at the jelly bean–less carpet. Just a big poppy. It was pretty, but looked drab without the added festive colors of FD&C Blue #1 and Yellow #5. Where had they all gone so fast?

Still, looking at my assignment book, it felt good to

cross another task off my list. I punched down the Publish button on my screen and then gasped. I had meant to publish this to Mr. Vandervart's Dropbox! I had accidentally opened up a blog post rather than a Word doc. I'd been so busy trying to keep my mind off the results of going public that it actually worked.

"Oh no, oh no, oh no," I groaned into my laptop. "I can't believe I just did that. Stupid, stupid, stupid!" I snagged the quilt off my bed and then crawled over to my desk drawer to pull out the package of M&M's. Bad news needed cushioning.

Typing my blog address into the menu bar, I held my breath when my three essays appeared. I saw the newest one at the top and scrolled down to my first blog entry. I scowled at the dreaded comments section below it. I can't believe blogs invited people to leave rude opinions once they finished reading. I'd totally forgotten. And had I remembered, I would've ditched the idea and run for cover. *Sure, Mom, I think your suggestion to write a public pudge profile rocks. It's bound to score me some popularity points.*

Ugh. I saw three comments. Summer had responded to my first blog entry. She'd said,

Pinkpetals: Opal, you are too funny. See you at school tomorrow.

Two more sat at the bottom of my second entry. One from a girl I didn't know. It said,

> **Cloud9:** I always "get sick" on the day of the President's Challenge. That way, I can do all the tests with my PE teacher after school as a makeup and my scores are totally private.

Wow. She might have something there.

G-pa had clearly written the last comment. He must have figured out how to surf the net. It said,

> **Graybeardgaffer:** IT'S A WASTE OF TIME MAKING KIDS EXERCISE. THEY SHOULD BE OUT IN THE STREETS WITH A TIN CAN AND A STICK. CHASE AFTER A BALL, FOR PETE'S SAKE. HOW MANY OF US WILL ACTUALLY HANG FROM THE ROOT OF A TREE HALFWAY DOWN A CANYON? THAT'S THE ONLY PERSON WHO'LL NEED TO PRACTICE THE FLEXED-ARM HANG. OH, AND MAYBE THE GUY WHO CAN'T HOLD HIS LIQUOR AND KEEPS SLIDING DOWN HIS BAR STOOL. HURTS LIKE THE DEVIL WHEN YOU WHACK YOUR CHIN.

I leaned back against my bed and let my head fall. That wasn't so bad. Not nearly bad. In fact, no one had slaughtered me like I thought they would. Of course, only my best friend, my grandfather, and some girl I didn't know had commented, but people had a chance and didn't take it. Maybe blogging wasn't as bad as I thought. And Summer had a point. No one in the school paid attention to me. Most kids didn't even know my name.

I raised my head and looked back at the screen. I scrolled up to my latest entry and did a double take. Three comments already!

Glamourgirl88: Opl, I totally agree with you. I need more veg time. I am sooo behind in my Runway Girls episodes I can't imagine I'll ever catch up. OMG, how could I live without free Wi-Fi? It's the only way I can keep up with my shows while I'm supposedly listening in class.

Umm, oops, I thought. Not exactly my point, but okay, whatever. The next comment caught me off guard,

Lovemycat: Dear Opl, why do you spell your name like that?

I scratched my head. Was I allowed to answer? Someone asks me a question on my blog and I can answer them back, right? It's my blog. I scrolled down to the last comment to read before making a reply.

My eyes popped out like two ping-pong balls. It felt like my eyelids had stretched to an unholy position. Summer's twin brother left a comment!

EthanEngland: You are such a crack up, "Opl."

I wanted to choke. I couldn't breathe. And then I couldn't stop panting. Ethan left a comment! Ethan Waldenbridge! The cutest, cutest, CUTEST boy in the eighth grade!

I rolled to the floor and pushed my laptop aside. A big groan crawled up my throat. I couldn't stop it. I did not recognize the sound, but I knew the feeling that came with it. Humiliation.

How could Summer have passed on my blog to her twin brother—the one person I would like never to notice me?

Well, that's not entirely true.

I don't want him to notice me when I'm spying on him with Summer at their house. And definitely not now, when Mom keeps reminding me I'm not some boney goddess in skinny jeans. And here? On my blog? Where I have been tricked into revealing things about myself? This is so not good.

I rolled my head to the side and looked for the package of M&M's. Ethan is my deepest, darkest secret.

When I first met Summer, after her family's move from the UK to America, I thought she was too good to be true. Not only did she like me and my loony sense of humor, but she didn't seem to mind that I had only three outfits I felt comfortable wearing. And none of them worth borrowing.

"You wear your personality like everyone else wears clothes. That's what I like about you. You're barmy," she had said a couple of years ago.

A couple of years ago, things had been really different. G-pa didn't live with us, Dad did, and I wasn't fat. It seems that as my size expanded, my personality shrank. It couldn't breathe beneath all the extra layers of flab that appeared. I felt like a turtle retracting into a shell. And Mom had thrown a laptop in there to play with.

Ethan was perfect. And he had Summer's sweet, foreign accent. I could be anywhere in school and hear him coming. Having an English accent brings a lot of luck your way. It makes you instantly popular, plus the teachers automatically give you thirty extra IQ points.

I practice my English accent daily, so that one day, when I'm married to Ethan, he'll understand me, and I can teach our children the proper way to speak. Someday.

I let my head fall to the side. I stared at my laptop on the floor beside me. I didn't want Ethan to think I was a crack up. I wanted him to think I was divine. I groaned the same groan I had been groaning for the last year only in different keys.

I got up to look in my dresser mirror. Who was this person? I didn't recognize her, but she had enveloped me. Like a hug I didn't want. That's it, I decided. I looked like my great-aunt Marge. She was all flabby arms and big bosom. An embrace from her left you gasping for air and with a muscle spasm. I refused to morph into someone named after a saturated fat.

I fell in a heap to the floor. Why couldn't I be normal again? Just regular. Ordinary. Run-of-the-mill. I looked at my fistful of M&M's and let them tumble out of my hand. How come I couldn't stop eating? I closed my mouth and pressed my lips together, but I knew this was stupid. I was still hungry. I needed to keep the noisy bits inside me fed to stay quiet. I just wanted to stop feeling all these feelings.

At first I had wanted everyone to stop looking at me because my dad died. Summer said they did it because they were offering sympathy, but I'm sure all they were doing was rubber-necking a crash site. It made me feel like a freak. Then I couldn't stop eating because somehow the food made me feel a little better, only it ended up making things worse. Now people are staring at me all over again. More gawking at my rear-ender. This sucks!

I wish I didn't care. I wish I didn't care about anything at all and that I had been born without emotions. Then I would never cry again. I would never be caught off guard when those hateful attacks gripped me and squeezed me. When my wall smashes and everything I kept squished down heaves upward from the floor of my guts.

I didn't want that anymore. I didn't want any of it.

I lifted my head from the carpet and looked at my laptop. The cursor blinked. It ticked like a silent clock, a reminder about the second comment which was really a question. *Dear Opl, why do you spell your name like that?*

I sighed. I might as well answer her. It would take my mind off the shock in the mirror.

Dear Lovemycat,

Last year, my seventh grade class had to come up with ways to become less wasteful. I'm trying to be more environmentally conscious and use less ink, so I cut a useless vowel. Also, my used electric typewriter lost its "A" key and gives a zingy shock when you press down on the spiky metal arm. I've been conditioned not to use it.

Okay, some of that was true, but most importantly, it made my name skinny, and I liked the sound of something linked to me having success with weight loss.

I punched Publish and shut my laptop. I needed relief from all the stress of this hard work and worry. Downstairs in the pantry lay a bag of hidden kettle corn with my name on it. Caramel is a sticky bandage, but it would make licking my wounds easier. Except first I had to pee.

Chapter
5

$\top$uesday morning, I sat at the breakfast table using
the palm of my hand to prop me up. I shook my
head, trying to clear my sleepy stupor and the vision
in front of me. Ollie, or someone with Ollie's face, was
dressed as a nurse. He shoveled cereal into his mouth as
if he believed someone was about to snatch the bowl out
from under him.

"Slow down, buddy," I mumbled. "Where's the fire?"

"I have to hurry," he said, bits of food flying from
his mouth. "I have to get to school before Jacob
Berndowser does."

My eyelids slid back into the *closed for the season* position. "How come?"

"As long as I make it to school before him, I'm safe.
He can't push me down at school. There are too many
teachers watching."

I raised one eyelid. "Why would he push you down?"

"He doesn't like my clothes." Ollie shrugged a white-cloaked shoulder and slapped a kiss on Mom's cheek as she placed a bowl of Cheerios in front of me.

"Hold on, Ollie," Mom said, but he'd dashed out the front door with his Spider-Man backpack. She put a hand on her hip and turned back to me. "What was that all about? Did he just say he was getting pushed down at school?"

I raised the other eyelid and reached for my spoon. "Haven't the foggiest. Well, maybe yes, I think so." I shoveled a load of cereal toward my mouth. I needed an extra bit of zip if I wanted to make it to school on time, but I doubted Cheerios could do the job. I missed the smell and taste of my regular Froot Loops—those jewel-toned spheres whose colors are so perky.

"I'll call his teacher," she sighed, shaking her head. Then she tapped the table in front of me. "But Ollie's costume reminded me that you have a doctor's appointment after school today. You're due for your yearly physical."

I shuddered. "Is it Dr. Killer again?"

Mom gave me *the face*. "No. It's not Dr. Quiller. He's retired."

"Quilled too many kids?"

"Opal!" She looked a bit prickly this morning. "No. This afternoon you'll see a new pediatrician. Her name is Dr. Beth Friedman. She's taking over his practice. You need to talk to her about this weight battle we've been dealing with."

I flinched at her words. A battle. "Will you be there?"

"Not this time. I'm buried in mounds of paperwork. I can't even get started on fixing up the shop. And I can't get anyone to help me either because I have no money to pay them. We're barely getting the bills paid as it is. There's so much to do inside, I don't know where to begin. An inch of dust and grime covers every flat surface." Mom shook her head and stared back at her desk. Then she mumbled, "Things just aren't going the way they're supposed to." She trudged back to her computer.

I looked at my Cheerios. They bobbed there in my milk like miniature life preservers. Maybe one day, if Mom did have things go her way, I could squeeze through one of those loops. I'll shrink enough until I'll no longer appear on her fix-it list.

⌒

It wasn't until lunch break that I saw Summer. We sat in our usual spot beneath the beech tree's big umbrella branches, and I spent most of the break griping about the new lunch menu. Earlier today we had been forced to sit through another dreadful "special seminar" event. We had been introduced to the new dining staff and their *exciting* and *monumental* ideas for the cafeteria overhaul.

They looked like the regular lunch ladies, the ones who have been here even since Mom went to school, but two new faces grinned among them. They stood shoulder to shoulder, faces scrubbed and shiny. Cheeks pink. Eyes crinkling with enthusiasm. We immediately stood on guard. G-pa said people that happy were usually in commercials trying to sell you junk.

When Principal Souresik came to the microphone to address the two hundred and fifty middle schoolers sitting in the bleachers, he gave us the face that suggested we'll really like this medicine. Even if it smelled like old socks and scratched our throats going down.

"Young ladies and gentlemen…" He always started his speeches this way. It was a bit like he was pretending to be the head of a better school, with a bigger stage and kids who hung on every one of his words. "I would like to introduce the two people responsible for our very own Meal Madness—the overhaul of school lunch programs created by the great Alfie Adam in England."

Meal Madness? The buzz in the bleachers sounded like a meadow full of drowsy bees.

"Alfie Adam has challenged America to make necessary changes in our schools for the health of our future generations. Changes that will make an impact on both our lunch lines and our waistlines. And from there we will see that a well-fed body makes a well-fed mind. It's the ripple effect we can all benefit from." I groaned. I couldn't believe it. Apparently our school had been sucked into the black hole of health too—just like the other schools around us.

I had no idea who this Alfie person was, but his fancy-pants plans had marched into our school and confused the staff. Or hypnotized them. The principal and the two people next to him all shared a shiny, glazed look on their faces, like my favorite doughnuts from Krispy Kreme.

The principal gestured at the couple. "Please welcome to our school the new heads of the dining hall, Chefs Jerry and Patricia Blackwell."

A trickle of polite applause came from the few teachers sprinkled throughout the bleachers. The two chefs moved forward to put their mouths close to the microphone. "Good morning, everyone," Chef Jerry said. He had massive white teeth, like a beaver with a good dentist. "We're very excited to join your community and hope we'll all be fast friends."

A variety of snorts and giggles rippled through the crowd.

"We know most of you have never expressed any

dissatisfaction with the cafeteria and may find the significant changes during the next months surprising. Don't be alarmed. We promise nothing will happen overnight. And chances are, by then, we'll have an overwhelming amount of support from you guys. Can't wait to see you in line. Come introduce yourselves. Chef Patricia and I have a lot in store for you."

One short hour later, Summer and I looked down at the trays holding our cafeteria food. Everything looked the same as always, apart from the shiny, red apple sitting in one of the compartments, too smug to be likable. I still had my cheese pizza, my french fries, my big square brownie, and my blue Gatorade. I'd forgotten to take my Hershey's syrup to school that morning, so I had to go with my second-choice drink.

I peeled the sticker off the apple and read the label aloud. "Organic Honey Crisp." I looked up at our beech tree. "I think you may have dropped this." I tossed the apple to the base of its trunk and then looked at Summer. "I never ordered that. Did you?"

She shook her head but took a bite from the one she held in her hand. Juice dribbled down her chin and she smiled. "Nope, but it's brilliant."

"I don't like these new people. No one can be that happy."

Summer rolled her eyes and crunched through another big bite.

"Who the heck is Adam Alfie anyway?"

"No. It's Alfie Adam."

"Does it matter? The guy has two first names. They're interchangeable. Who does that to their baby?"

"He's wicked in England."

I nodded. "I'll bet. Soon enough he'll be hated here too."

Summer laughed and almost choked on her too-perfect-to-actually-eat apple. She looked like Snow White with her ivory skin and dark hair—which wasn't quite dark enough to qualify as ebony, so I called it light black. Clearly, she'd fallen for the evil queen's traditional trick, giving us poisonous apples meant to entice the innocent. "No," she coughed and laughed together. "He's wicked as in wicked brilliant. He's loved in England."

"Loved for what? Sucking the joy out of lunch? He's taken away our flavored milks! That was the healthy stuff, right? Milk builds strong bones? He's now responsible for my early onset of osteopo-something-er-other."

She squinted at me.

"Brittle bones."

Summer snorted. "Aflie Adam made English schools change their lunch menus. He's now in charge of this program that's sweeping through schools everywhere. In

England, they used to serve children horrible, scrappy food you shouldn't even feed your pets. Now they give kids fab food."

"Fab food," I echoed.

"Yep. You should check him out on the web. He's the Nude Food Dude."

"What? Ewww!" I reeled back.

Summer smiled at me, the adult smile she'd perfected from watching the queen, I'm sure. The one that said, *You plebeians will never understand how we brilliant monarchs think. Just trust me.* "Seriously, Opal. Check him out. I absolutely adore him. He's one of my heroes." She picked up her tray to head back inside, but I held up a hand.

"Wait. Speaking of the web, how could you have sent my blog on to your brother?"

Her eyebrows lifted and hid beneath her hairline. "I told you I'd already sent it on to a bunch of people—and I've already said sorry. Stop worrying, Opal, your stuff is brill. You're fun to read. And he promised not to let anyone know it's you." She waved good-bye and left me thinking. About Ethan, my blog, and now this naked guy who persuaded my principal that cooking without clothing is not only sanitary, but fab fun.

Chapter

6

After school let out, I walked the five blocks down our old-fashioned Main Street to the pediatrician's office I'd been visiting my entire thirteen years of life. I knew the two nurses, I knew the receptionist, and I'd known Dr. Killer for probably a few more seconds than I'd known Mom. All known, all knowing, and no surprises. A new doctor was like a pop quiz—suddenly your heart bams up against your rib cage and your sweat glands release the floodgates.

Would this Dr. Beth woman wear something theme related the way Dr. Killer had done? I guess he'd thought dressing like a cast member from the circus would distract from his poking and prodding. Or maybe he'd left because the Ringling brothers finally offered him a job.

I waited in the examining room on the long slab of crinkly paper, legs swinging wildly, and gazed at the whales, octopi, and other sea creatures stenciled onto the walls. I should have brought my snorkel. Except the room did not smell at all like the seashore. More like the stinging, bleachy scent of our neighborhood pool after too many little kids had peed in it. And this reminded me that I had to use the bathroom.

Three soft knocks on the door must have been the magic code to get it to swing open. A young woman with thick, black rectangular frames surrounding her speckled, brown eyes sailed into the room. I caught a quick peek at her face before she ducked down into my medical folder. "Opal Oppenheimer, right? Have I said that correctly?"

I shrugged. I wasn't going to be too helpful. She'd order something with a needle in it sooner or later.

She flipped over the page in front of her. My weight and height graph. She sat down in Dr. Killer's squeaky wheelie chair and rolled in front of me. "It's nice to meet you. I'm Beth Friedman. You can call me Beth." She put out her hand to shake mine.

I looked at her. Where was the all-important *Doctor* bit? Was she truly a doctor? She looked like she should be my babysitter. I shook her hand. "Hi," I said. She had no gimmicky clothing. Just faded green scrubs under her white lab coat.

Her skin wrinkled in the forehead area. She leaned back in her chair and took off her chunky glasses. "You remind me of a girl I saw in a movie once."

I nodded. "Little Miss Sunshine," I said. I'd heard that before. I'd not been allowed to see it yet. Maybe she swore a lot in the film. Or got naked. How horrible. I would never do that. I won't even look at myself naked in my bathroom mirror, so I can't imagine allowing millions of moviegoers to take a crack at it first. "Are you going to tell me I'm fat?"

"Well, actually I was about to say that movie makes my all-time favorites list because of the girl. Do you ask everyone you just meet that question?" She looked at me with a little twinkle in her eye. Or maybe it was a piece of dirt.

"No. But I thought you'd want to get down to business like my other doctor did. He always asked questions and never listened to the answers. I heard the same ones each visit. Ten in all. I'd most often answer the first two, like 'How are you?' and 'How's school?' But then, when I knew he'd already tuned me out, I changed things up a bit."

The dirt must have still been in her eye, except that she smiled along with the squint. "How?"

I leaned back on the wrinkled paper. "Like when he asked about my little brother, I told him that because we were low on cash, Mom had sold him on the black market. And now he worked in a Mexican sweatshop for a man named the Big Tamale. Or when he asked about my latest hobbies, I'd said I liked to iron and I'd started growing my own furniture."

Beth pressed her lips together, but her eyes stayed wrinkly. "I like your style, kiddo."

"Do you mean my talent to lie or this particular big, fat fib?"

"The latter. The former will get you some serious black marks one day, but if you're prepared to take the heat, then I think you've got a future in politics."

"Great," I said. "Then maybe I can change the law regarding the criminal behavior taking place in our school's cafeteria."

"What's going on?" No crinkle this time, but her eyebrows skyrocketed northward.

"No fun food."

"Describe fun food."

I sighed. "You know, doughnuts, potato chips, soda, chocolate. That sort of thing."

She nodded. "Ah yes, fun food. It's nice to have those once in a while."

"I find once in a while doesn't cut it."

She leaned back in that squeaky chair. "No? How come?"

"Well, they make me feel better. They kinda soften most of my problems."

"What sorts of problems are you having?"

I rolled my eyes. "I have to pee all the time. I'm so tired, I'd give my left lung to stay in bed most days. And things are super prickly at home."

Beth put my chart down on the desk and shook her head. "I've been hearing that a lot lately."

"Really?"

"Yup. You'd be surprised to know how many kids come through our doors wrestling with these very same things."

I narrowed my eyes at her. "Is there some sort of injection you give as a treatment?"

"Nope. But there are plenty of things that can help. I've got a few you might want to consider."

I kept my eyes in the narrowed position and didn't respond.

"Let me guess. When you go into a slump and want to escape, I bet you feel like zoning out in front of the tube, eating a pile of junk food, and crawling beneath the covers. And chances are you don't want to come out from beneath them, right?"

I nodded an inch.

She shrugged. "We all get like that sometimes. But you might be surprised to know about something that can reverse those feelings. A little exercise."

"I hate sports. I'm no good at them, so cross that off your list."

"Exercise isn't just athletics, Opal. I'm just talking about getting your body moving. And moving produces endorphins. I call these happy hormones. They make us feel good again."

"It's hard to feel good in my house."

"Why?"

"Well, according to my mom, I need to lose weight. She hates that I'm fat." My face pinched into its perfected Sour Patch Kids mold.

Beth shook her head. "I'm not so fond of that word. It's quite the zinger to one's confidence."

"Well, she's *confident* I'm fat—and *confident* she wants me skinny."

She chewed on her lip for a second. "Are you sure your mom wants you to be skinny or just take off some weight and become healthier?"

"She's clipping out pictures of models who would put a sapling to shame."

Beth nodded her head.

"Diet food fills up the shelves in our house. Diet cookies, diet cake, diet ice cream, diet candy. And they don't taste half-bad, but they're not doing anything. She wants you to fix it."

Beth chuckled. "I can't fix it, Opal, but I can help you. You're the only one in charge here. You're the one who's going to make the changes that will produce some results."

I grunted. "I've had lots of change lately. None of it's been good in the result department."

She glanced back at my chart and nodded. "I agree, some changes are unwelcome ones, but what I have in mind might help out a little. Like I said, moving your body around will be a good start." She put up a hand to stop me from objecting. "Now I'm not talking about joining the track team. Just hear me out. It sounds like you could use something for both your body and your mind. Have you heard of yoga?"

My face went back into scrunch mode. "Yoga? Sure, but isn't it more like a religion?"

Beth smiled and showed her tiny white teeth. They looked like a row of Tic Tacs. "Not entirely. It's more like an individual practice, although you often do it in a class with other students. But it's not competitive. It's not a sport. Everyone works on their own bodies and minds."

"How can you work on your mind? It sounds too much like school."

Beth shook her head. "Not at all. It's more an attitude about life. You might enjoy it."

I wasn't so sure. Being taught an attitude sounded about as fun and fast as chiseling a statue of myself out of rock. And with nothing more than a soup spoon. It might be quicker to have a shot. I needed a speedy cure. "Where is this yoga?"

Beth looked at her watch and got up, warming her stethoscope with her breath. She started the official exam. "There's a studio not far from here. I'll give your mom the address."

"Are we almost done?" She checked inside my ears but wasn't digging in quite as far as Dr. Killer used to. He always went in up to his elbow.

"Right after you pee in a cup."

I reeled. "Pee in a cup?"

"Uh-huh," she mumbled, finishing up the search in my ears. "And tomorrow morning, jump back in here before school, before you have any breakfast, and we'll draw a little blood."

"What? How come? Nurses usually just poke me with a needle to put stuff in, not take it away."

Beth put a warm hand on my shoulder. "Sorry, kiddo. I know it's not very pleasant, but we need to check out a few things. You can't eat for eight hours before we take the blood sample, so promise me you'll pack your breakfast and eat it *after* the visit. It'll just take a second. And when I get the results back, I'll have a conversation with your mom about the icky diet foods she's asking you to eat."

I panicked a little. "You're not going to ask her to get rid of everything are you? Because I *need* food. I'm hungry all the time."

Beth gave my hand a soft squeeze. "No, honey. Not everything. But there are much better alternatives to what you have right now. Plus, I'm not so sure it's food you're actually hungry for."

My mood was like a droopy balloon but puffed up a tiny bit when I heard that. No more diet food. Fabeedodah. Still, I hadn't wanted to end my day peeing in a cup and knowing one of the vampire nurses would soon suck my blood out. Not that I couldn't supply them with plenty of the first one. I'd been sitting cross-legged for the last twenty minutes, desperate for relief. I would find mood relief at home. I'd have to check my supply of Oreos. Those guys will surely make this big ol' blimp of blues float a little higher.

Daisychaingirl: Dear Opl,

The guy who sits next to me in homeroom makes my life miserable. He's constantly passing gas—on purpose! I swear this isn't a situation where he has some sort of health problem. The guy actually does it on command and then laughs about it. He's horrible!

I figured since you posted a lot about school, you might have a good way of dealing with this.

Fed up with farts,

Daisychaingirl

I sat back against the pillows propped up on my bed's headboard and nibbled on a fingernail. I hadn't expected anyone to write me for advice. This was tricky. What did I know about other people's problems? I wasn't a therapist, I thought to myself. But I suppose it was nice to know I wasn't the only one with a daily can of worms.

I scribbled a few notes on a piece of paper, Googled a few things, and went to work writing my response. After an hour, I scrolled up to reread my reply.

Dear Daisy,

This situation "reeks" of deception. Most of the boys in my class are totally fascinated with every bodily noise they can pump out, and the ability to butt bark at a moment's notice has probably earned the creep a big bonus with the rest of the guys.

Just out of curiosity, I did a little research. I found

out that the average person creates about half a liter of colon cologne each day. Also, fartrogen dioxide has been clocked at speeds of around seven mph. I even found out that the Roman Emperor Claudius once passed an edict making farting legal at banquets. (That is so gross.)

Sadly, no one can put a ban on intentional flatulence.

Might he be trying to get your attention? Maybe he wants you to notice him and doesn't realize that his methods are backfiring. (No pun intended.)

How about you place a portable air freshener on the corner of your desk closest to him? If he doesn't take the hint, then squirt him with a spray bottle full of water on stream. That's what we do with our hairy hound when he sits beneath the kitchen table releasing his potent canine fumes. Even if it doesn't stop him, at least he'll get up to go do it somewhere else.

Sometimes you just have to find the right language to make an impact.

Good luck,

Opl

I pressed Publish and nearly shut my laptop when I remembered Summer's suggestion about looking up this clothingless cook. My stomach squinched just thinking about it. I didn't want this flashy froufrou change in our lunch program. It was fine the way it was.

I typed in Wikipedia and discovered several things. Firstly, I'm guessing the photographer, to my great relief, must have insisted this guy put on some clothes. Maybe it's Wikipedia's rule because kids use the site for researching their homework. Secondly, this guy has worked a lot. In fact, all around the world. He's a super-famous chef. I can't believe there are so many people who want to eat food cooked by a naked person. I bet he travels light.

After reading for a few more minutes, I came across the best piece of info. He does *not* cook in the nude. Apparently, only his grub is garmentless. As in, not smothered with stuff that hides its real look and taste. *How hard is that?* I thought. Any goon can lay an apple on your lunch tray and shout "Ta-da!" But this guy gets paid big bucks to do it.

Reading his biography left my eyes crooked. He'd done a whole bunch of things with his life and almost all of them had to do with food. When you looked at it that way, he was my kind of guy. Except he squelched the most important food group. Fast food. Did he not realize how necessary this was to our culture? America cannot survive without our double arches. We would fail at success, because we'd arrive late to everything. Fast food means Want it, Get it, Eat it, Go. This explains our country's superpower attitude. We don't have to waste time waiting for the water to boil.

My chest grew tight reading about his seizure of English lunchrooms and attempts to overhaul their menus of fish and chips. I read that in one school, after the Lunch Grinch took charge, a group of parents started delivering junk food to kids through the school's playground fence as a revolt against his dishes.

And that's when I came across his poisonous Meal Madness plan…for America. He planned to do the same to American children that he'd done to the English. Forcing buckets of naked food down our gullets without any ketchup to accompany it!

I tried unclenching my fists as I stared at Alfie Adam's face. It smiled at me from the screen. A more truthful picture would be him standing in front of a crowd of skinny, sad children, sticking his tongue out at them. Why were perfect people always telling you how to live your life so you could be perfect just like them?

I clicked on the link to his website and watched his YouTube video about the evils of junk food and how it didn't belong in kids' diets. I was ready for a shouting match. I watched. I listened.

The man was a little pudgy.

He stuttered a bit.

His hair was a mess.

They didn't show anything below his knees, but I bet if they had, I'd have seen he had two left feet. This man was a celebrity and *not perfect*.

I smiled and bit down on a giggle. He came across different than I thought he would. Maybe he wasn't so bad.

"Aaahhhh!" I shouted and jumped from my bed. "Consorting with the enemy. That's what they want!" If he could sucker me in with just a funny accent and a goofy face, then I was no better than the rest of them.

Except I love funny accents and goofy faces.

Well, I'd just have to stay strong. My Nutter Butters had been there for me, and I would not let the people working for Nabisco suffer any boycott. Maybe I would even eat extras to help make up for those kids in England. I thought we'd all suffered enough.

Chapter

7

The next day after school, I congratulated myself for making it to Diggerman's without tripping in front of the soup kitchen guy. In fact, I was so busy thinking about how I wouldn't let Alfie Adam make me feel guilty for eating *un*-naked food that I waltzed right passed him. Never even saw him. But I knew he was there.

What I did see when I came home were two brown paper grocery bags on the kitchen counter. I loved grocery day. It had been a hard day at school with the dreadful morning blood test on an empty stomach, two quizzes, and a lunch that included plain milk and Snow White's apple again. I'd left mine for the busy, nut-gathering squirrels. They liked tree food. I'm more Mickey D food. But right now, I wanted the prizes that came from those grocery bags. The supermarket offered flashy-colored boxes with pictures of crunchy, salty, syrupy sweet food plastered on them. I opened the bag and rifled through the goods. What was this? This wasn't our regular stuff.

I pulled out a bunch of vegetables. Green ones, brown ones, some red guys, and something either brown or purple or both. It was brurple. And on the bottom, I spotted a bag I'm guessing the school sent home. Apples. Probably the ones I threw out. Couldn't have that, could we? We must make all students suffer equally.

"G-pa?" I called out into the living room. "What's all this stuff in here?"

"A good start," he growled back.

I walked over to his chair. "I don't get it. What's a good start?"

He put the flap down over his laptop and turned to look at me. "Broccoli, red peppers, eggplant, onions. It's a good start to better health."

I felt my insides scrunch up. "Better health looks like all the fun got sucked out of it."

"Better health gives you a better shot at having fun." He swung his slippered feet off Mr. Muttonchops, who didn't mind being an ottoman. "Let's get going." He pulled himself out of his chair and waited for a few joints to crack into place, then pointed toward the bags on the counter. "Dinner isn't going to make itself."

I looked back toward the kitchen. "No. It waits for Mom."

"Not tonight, sweetheart. Tonight, you will learn all about the mysteries of the Orient."

"Are you talking about that shiny blob on the counter? The Orient doesn't look edible."

G-pa grunted and shuffled past me. "That's an eggplant. And you'll soon change your mind about its taste—no matter what it looks like. It's a guest star in our stir-fry tonight. I don't often throw them in, but it begged to join the others in my grocery cart, so I gave in."

"I would have resisted."

"Well, after supper you may be singing a different tune."

"I like the one I have been singing. Where's the pizza? Tonight's supposed to be pizza night. Monday and Thursday are the fat-free hot dogs and Tater Tots. Tuesday and Friday are low-fat chicken nuggets and canned peaches. Wednesday and Saturday are pizza night and non-fat cottage cheese. And Sunday we drive-thru at McDonald's as my reward for eating all the diet stuff. This is Wednesday. Where's the pizza?"

"That garbage isn't pizza. Pizza doesn't taste or look like the gunk your mother brings home and stores in the freezer. I'm cooking tonight. Scratch that. *We're* cooking tonight. Now go grab an apron and wash your hands."

My lower jaw fell to my belly button and would have stayed there had G-pa not pointed with an extra pointy finger toward the pantry where the aprons hung. I turned around and went to choose one. They looked brand-new. Not a spot of food on any of them. Except for the one Dad used to use.

I plucked his off the hook and smoothed it down the front of me. It said, *Dijon Vu—The feeling you've had mustard before.* I washed my hands and heard G-pa make swashbuckling sword sounds with a long knife and something that looked like a silver stick. "What are you doing?" The sound was dangerous, but I wanted to hear more of it.

"Sharpening our tools."

"Aren't they safer if they're dull?"

"Nope. In fact, the dull ones are the most dangerous kind. They slip off your food and onto your hands."

I nodded. "That's why I say we wait and let Mom make dinner. She knows just how to open the plastic on the freezer pizza so she won't get cut. I don't mind waiting."

G-pa shook his head. "Sorry, girlie. Now get me the kitchen stool and come over to the cutting board. Pay attention. Knife skills are important."

After twenty minutes of sleeping with my eyes open, I glanced at the pile of colorful vegetables he had scooped into a giant dish. Evenly cubed, they waited beside a plastic bowl of onions that had made both of us tear up as he'd diced them. He grabbed a big frying pan from a cupboard below the cutting board and filled it with a few spoonfuls of oil. Twisting a knob on the stove lit a blue flame beneath the pan. Within thirty seconds, the scent of something dark and smoky came to my nose. "What do I smell?" I asked.

"Toasted sesame oil," G-pa answered. "Addictive once you develop the taste for it." He threw the onions into the pan and had me mix. Then bit by bit he added the other vegetables and told me to keep stirring so nothing would burn.

I saw him head back into the pantry and come out with a bag of rice. The rice grains reminded me of the insects you'd find under a dead log. "We're not going to eat those, are we?"

G-pa poured a cup of the dead white bugs into a pot with some water and threw in some salt. "You will if you know what's good for you."

"Well, it's a good thing I know better than to eat something that looks like a bunch of dead bugs."

He gave me one of his scrunched up faces. "This is rice, Opal. You should know that by now. Haven't you ever had rice?"

"It's in the boxes Ollie and I always throw away after Mom's ordered from the Kung Pao Palace."

G-pa tsked. "What a waste. Rice is good for you. I've been blathering on to your mom about this for the last year. She's been too soft on you guys and too busy, buying all those freezer box foods and takeout muck. You kids need a change of food."

Ollie skipped into the kitchen wearing my Hermione witch costume from last Halloween. "We're having a change of food? You mean it's not pizza night?"

I looked at him a little glumly, even though the gunk in the pan smelled good. "We're having rice. It's come all the way from China." *Although it looks like it died trying to get here.*

Ollie twirled to make the cape float around him. "I love Chinese people. They get to eat with sticks."

G-pa nodded. "Chopsticks. But I don't have any tonight, so you'll have to make do with a fork."

"How 'bout I go get some from outside?" Ollie asked, but G-pa shook his head with a smile.

"When did you learn how to cook?" I asked G-pa. He searched a shelf by the stove and pulled out little jars, tipping bits of dried leaves into my vegetable pan as I stirred.

"I was stationed in Yokosuka during my service in the military. Army food stinks, so I started searching elsewhere for grub. The Japanese knew how to handle food. I paid attention."

The red peppers sizzled in the oil as I poked at them. "The Japanese taught you?"

"Well, I watched how the men and women cooked."

Ollie tilted his head and his witch's cap slid to point at the floor. "I thought only girls cooked. That's my costume for tomorrow—a big flowery apron."

G-pa wagged a finger. "Some of the greatest chefs in the world are men. Even your dad cooked, remember?" He sighed at Ollie's shaking head. "All men should know how to cook."

I thought about Alfie Adam and his scruffy hairdo. "All men should know how to comb their hair too."

G-pa gave me a crooked look. "You two set the table while I finish up the rice."

Ollie danced with the dishes and hummed a song about how wonderful everything smelled. I put out the forks and glasses and then set the big jug of chocolate milk on the table.

"None of that junk tonight. We're drinking water. Chocolate milk will ruin the flavor of the food," G-pa barked.

"Water?" I said. "Water is for washing dishes."

"Soy sauce will make you thirsty. And since you're way too young for sake, water is the next best thing."

I grumbled under my breath but filled the glasses at the

sink and then sat down just as G-pa came over with two plates. The rice looked white and fluffy and made a bowl for the vegetables to sit in. The onions, eggplant, and peppers were mixed in with bright green broccoli and covered in a glossy, brown sauce.

"What's this?" Ollie asked, holding up one of the miniature trees.

"Broccoli," G-pa said as he put his plate down across from mine. "I'm guessing that also got tossed along with the rice?" He clucked his tongue again and pulled a bottle of dark brown liquid from his shirt pocket and slid it in front of my plate. "Try this. You'll like it. Just sprinkle it over the stir-fry."

"The what?" Ollie said with a mouthful of food.

"Stir-fry. It's what we made. We stirred a batch of frying vegetables and spooned them over white rice. It's a classic."

I put a drop onto my spoon and dipped a finger into the liquid. Salty. Bright. Tangy.

"What do you taste?" G-pa asked.

"It's brackish," I said. We were "Exploring Earth's Oceans" in our science unit.

"Good word." He winked at me.

"What's brackish?" Ollie asked, spooning another heapfull into his mouth.

"Like the sea. Marine-like," I explained.

"That's my costume for Friday. Ariel, the mermaid. She's marine life."

"I said marine-*like*."

"That's wrong," he said, licking his plate clean of the soy sauce. "It's the navy who like the sea."

G-pa tapped Ollie's plate. "Want some more?"

Ollie put his plate down and wiped his mouth with the back of his hand. "Can girls be army people?"

G-pa sat back. "Yep. But there weren't too many of them around when I worked in the service. Things have changed quite a bit since then though. Why?"

Ollie closed his eyes. "Shoot. I don't think I have anything to wear that's army looking for a girl."

I groaned. "Ollie, why don't you try wearing a few things meant for boys? It might help you."

He shook his head and took his plate to the sink. "I don't need any help. It's Mom who needs the help."

G-pa shrugged and made a face that said, *don't bother*, but just then Mom came through the front door and whooped out loud. "Dad, you are the best! This is perfect."

"Go scoop your mother up some supper, kiddo," he said to me.

When she sat down after dumping her things on her

desk, she looked exhausted but grateful. She turned to G-pa. "Did you tell her?"

"Tell me what?" I asked, eyeing both of them.

G-pa shook his head and rose from the table. "I'll deliver good food, not bad news."

"Thanks a lot," Mom said as he went into the kitchen to start cleaning up.

The white rice churned in my stomach. Even though dinner tasted great going down, I knew from experience it wouldn't be as good coming back the other way. "What bad news? Is something wrong?"

Mom bit her lip and put a hand across mine on the table. "We have to make some changes. Specifically, *you* have to make some changes, but we're all going to help. And the changes will help all of us too."

I hated double-talk. She wasn't making any sense. "You're getting me super worried. I've had to deal with enough changes in the last couple of years and none of them have helped any of us. What's the bad news?"

"Dr. Friedman called. She said you're prediabetic."

"*Prediabetic?* What does this mean?" I knocked back my chair trying to stand. "Am I going to die?"

Mom shook her head hard and then grabbed my hand again. "No," she said firmly. "No. Nothing like that. But we can't dismiss diabetes."

I pulled my hand out of hers. "I disagree. Our teacher talked about it in health class; it's not welcome here. I say we shove it out."

Mom sighed and sat back in her chair. She closed her eyes which were puffy and a bit smeared with mascara. "Opal, you're not making this easy for me. Please just be quiet and listen." Her eyes opened and I could tell she was at that glistening, watery stage right before your tears spilled over your bottom eyelids. And I could tell she fought to keep them inside. She tilted her head toward the ceiling to look up there while talking. "People develop diabetes when their body can't use sugar normally."

"I use sugar just fine. I've had loads of practice."

Mom shook her head. "It's not quite the same, Opal. When a doctor suspects someone has this condition, they do a test. Dr. Friedman said your test came back high and it needs to come down." She stopped while a tear rolled down her cheek.

I sat back down. My brain spun around the conversation I'd had with Dr. Friedman. "I don't understand this test thing. Doesn't higher mean better?" My face grew hot.

Mom wiped her eyes with the sleeve of her shirt. "No, honey. It's not a test like that. The test measures the amount of sugar in your blood."

I thought about the extra candy bar I ate before I had

gone to bed last night. That's probably what did it. I should have had the bag of potato chips instead. I admitted this to Mom.

"No," she said, "It's not sugar that shows up from something you've just eaten. Dr. Friedman says it's buildup. Months of sugar show up—not just the day's."

Whoa. Months of sugar? My eyes went wide. I thought about my daily trip to Diggerman's. The last few months had been pretty bad. I imagined all my purchases in a mound on the floor of my bedroom. Then I piled over that all of the things I'd snuck from the pantry. I topped it off with everything Mom allowed me as part of my "reward" for eating the icky diet food. It wasn't surprising it would show up in my blood. I suppose it had been leaking out of my stomach and had nowhere else to go.

"Okay," I said, "I'll eat less candy. How much less should I eat?"

Mom shook her head. "It's not just candy. Dr. Friedman sent me to a website that explained everything about diabetes. I'm finding out that sugar is in a lot of the other food we have around here too."

Mom looked dreadful. Like when the teacher hands back a test and you see their red pen writing with your number grade on the paper, and it says you got a ninety-nine, but then you realize you've read it upside down and it's actually a sixty-six. Sucker punched. "What are we going to do?" I asked.

Mom sighed and wiped at her tears again. "Whatever we have to. Grandpa has already decided to help cook some meals at home. We'll work together on the food. And the other stuff too."

I felt a zing of worry leap up my spine. "What other stuff?"

"Exercise. You're supposed to start exercising."

"Wait a second," I started in. "That doctor told me yoga wasn't exercise."

Mom shrugged. "I suppose. She did mention that as an option. Most importantly, she emphasized the need for you to get moving."

I bristled. "I do move!" I could feel heat burning in my cheeks, rushing through my whole face. Of course Mom would say something like this. She's way too busy with work to even look at me to see me moving.

Mom closed her eyes and pursed her lips. She took a breath and went on. "Dr. Friedman also thinks the yoga classes would help out with the stresses you're handling at the moment." She put her head into her hands and mumbled, "I sure wish I had something to handle all *my* stress. I'm desperate for an extra pair of hands. When is all this bad luck going to turn around?"

However I made it back to my room, I can't remember. But an hour later, I sprawled on my bed, feeling very sorry for myself. Warm tears slid down the sides of my face and made miniature pools inside my ears. It warped the sounds of my crying. Made my hiccups dull and whale-like. I was a National Geographic special. The Wailing Whale. Sounds of newly discovered marine life in a state of despair.

I thought about homework. Too much of it. I considered the Snicker bar on my shelf, but then glared at it. Why was this happening to me? I acted nicely to people. I made my bed. I vacuumed the living room when asked. I made sure Mr. Muttonchops's water bowl was always clean and his food bowl always full. I let Ollie borrow whatever clothes he wanted, mostly because they didn't fit me anyway, so somebody should use them. And I've only been to the principal's office twice. Once because I sneezed and my big pink wad of watermelon flavored Bubblicious flew into Suzie Sellerman's hair. And the other time because Josh Gruber stole my gym shorts from my backpack and made a flag with them at break. I had to chase him around the outside basketball courts and *accidentally* kneed him in the stomach as I reached up for them. I wasn't a person prediabetes should happen to.

Kids who got diseases were on telethons and had fire-men holding out their boots for you to fill with change. I was thirteen-year-old Opl Oppenheimer who had more than enough on my plate—except for the food variety. And now suddenly, my life was roaring down the road in the wrong direction. Devoid of Dad. Dumpy and distended. And now diseased.

I pulled my laptop over and logged on to Alfie Adam's website. There was a picture of Alfie, his wife, and his new son, Bobby Booboo. Five minutes later I could stand it no more. I opened a new blog page.

What's in a name? The famous question Shakespeare asked us to consider. I ask, What were they think-ing? This seems the right question for anyone having finished reading the article in a British news-paper all about Alfie Adam's newest baby, Bobby Booboo Archibald Adam. Now before any of you start writing me comments telling me that having a name like Bobby Booboo is not so horrible a crime, and maybe I ought to keep my big trap shut, let me release the names of his three daughters. The ones born before Bobby Booboo. First there's Maya Papaya Honeypot Adam. Then Daffydill Bluebell Lila Adam. And of course, who could forget Maple

Mary Puddin' Pie Adam? I think nobody will. I think saddled with these names, the children will find it impossible to avoid attention. They will also find it impossible to locate a spot at a lunch table. Or be picked for a dodgeball team. Or secure employment. Or look in the mirror.

Alfie Adam has it in for all children. He must hate us. So much so, he will ruin childhood for as many of us as he can put his oven-mitted hands on. This Lunch Grinch, from here on known as the Grunch, should not be in charge. In fact, I don't think he should be allowed to name farm animals.

But maybe he's getting back at his own parents for giving him two first names. And so now the line of punishment continues and he refuses to give any of his children first names. Maybe his head spends too much time inside gas ovens every day. Fumes can overwhelm the senses. I'm guessing his wife must be a cook too, and exposed to the same dangerous vapors. I can't imagine allowing my husband to name our babies something that either belongs on a salad or in an episode of *Sesame Street.*

Or maybe he just cooks super well and his wife loves his food so much she doesn't complain about the goofy names. But she's going to have to face the music soon. Shortly, her children will gang up on her and demand to know why their dad punished them. Why he saddled them for life. They're going to ask why she didn't stop him. And why he won't give them any McDonald's.

My hands launched full speed ahead. They attacked the keyboard like drumsticks on a snare. I stopped typing. If the Grunch had not been born, I would have chocolate and strawberry milk at school. I would be eating a Snickers bar right now. And I would have had pizza tonight.

I thought about the soy sauce. The vegetables in sesame oil. The broccoli and rice we used to toss into the garbage. G-pa's dinner wasn't horrible, but it was different than what I was used to. And I liked what I had before. Every time something changed it was always for a bad reason. Two years ago, someone flicked a giant finger at my carefully constructed domino snake and the sound of clicking tiles refused to stop.

A knock on my door brought me out of my fuming daze. Mom's head poked through the crack. "Can I come in? I have something for you." She made her way to my bed and sat on the edge of it. From her pocket she pulled a crumpled piece of paper. "Here's the address for the yoga class. Dr. Friedman said she thought it was well taught. And that you don't have to know anything about yoga because it's multilevel."

"What does that mean?" I asked, taking the address from her.

"Just that people who are brand-new to the course and those who know what they're doing are mixed together. It means the teacher will explain things to any new students as she goes along."

I sighed. "Will you come with me?"

Mom shook her head. "I have to work."

I glared at her. "Opening a bookshop takes forever."

"You could always pitch in and help," she said, raising her eyebrows.

I thought about all the cleaning and heavy lifting, and that all I'd end up doing was speeding up Mom's wish to spend more time away from us being much happier in her book world rather than her real world. I bet all the books in the kids' section were going to be about skinny, cheerful children.

"No thanks," I said sourly.

"There's a lot I don't know, and chances are it'll end up a big bust with no one coming. I'm sorry I can't go to yoga, Opal. But Grandpa said he'd go."

"G-pa?" I snorted. "You're joking."

"He said he'd try it until you feel okay going on your own. He'll probably be just as uncomfortable as you, so maybe you can focus on helping him if he needs it."

A picture of G-pa in leotards flashed through my mind. "When do we have to go?"

"The classes are twice a week for an hour. Mondays and Thursdays. You go tomorrow after school."

I groaned and fell back against my pillows.

Mom tapped my computer. "What are you working on?"

"I'm plotting ways to destroy the life of a chef because he is determined to spoil mine."

"Who's spoiling yours?"

"Alfie Adam."

"You mean the nude guy?" she said, stifling a giggle.

I whipped my head around to scowl at her. "He's not naked! He doesn't cook in the nude."

Mom shrugged. "I know that Opal. I was only kidding. How is he ruining your life?"

I sat up. "He's taking over school cafeterias. First he plotted against his own country's children, and now he's picking on the youth of America. He's determined to strip the world of burgers and fries."

"Well, maybe he can help you get into those cute jeans we talked about."

I glared at her. "*You've* talked about it! I don't need any stupid jeans!"

Mom's eyes went wide. "Whoa, Opal. What's all this about?"

Everything went suddenly blurry and shimmering like when I opened my eyes underwater. "You don't even see me anymore, do you? You don't look at me or listen to me." All that extra water finally spilled over my lower eyelids. "I'm not Opal to you…I'm OVAL!"

Mom stood up, her cheeks blazing. "How can you say that?"

"It's true! And you know what?" I said, reaching over for the Snickers bar. "I'm going to go right on being Oval. I don't even care about this stupid diabetes thing. Like you don't even care about me!" I ran into my bathroom and slammed the door, sliding down the inside of it and squishing the bar in my fist.

I waited there for five minutes until my heart stopped thudding. I flung open the door to see if Mom was still there, but she'd gone. Probably downstairs to rid our house of anything I liked—just to get back at me.

I slumped back down on my bed and looked at my blog. Mom had typed a message on the screen. It said, *Opal, I love you.*

I backspaced each letter. Delete. Delete. Delete. It was like erasing the whole conversation.

Then I looked at my blog post and wished I could erase Alfie Adam. I huffed. "Anyone who gives their children names like Muppets needs a few weeks in shock therapy." I should have signed it Miss Piggy, but chickened out. Instead I punched the Publish button.

Chapter 8

The next day I didn't see Summer for the whole morning. Not even passing in the halls. Where was she? My sour mood from last night required tending to and Summer was the only one who truly understood me. I *needed* her. She always pulled me right out of my basement blues and up to the level where I started making her laugh. We just learned about symbiotic relationships in science class, and that totally explained us. We acted like two fish feeding off of one another.

Finally, at lunchtime, I went to our beech tree and collapsed onto the picnic table's bench. I craned my neck around to view the mass of wandering students. She was always there before I was. She was always super on time. Summer hates to be late.

I ate my sandwich on my own, still waiting to catch a glimpse of a head with light black hair weaving its way through the student body, but after twenty minutes I gave up. I gathered my tray to take back inside, figuring Summer must have called in sick today. Now who did I have to moan to?

I yanked at the sticky door to the cafeteria, wrenching my shoulder and knocking over the rest of my lunch as the door suddenly gave way. The red plastic tray clattered to the ground along with my garbage and that ever-present red apple. Summer came through the door, spotted me fuming on the ground, and strutted past.

"Summer!" I twisted to look after her.

She stopped but didn't turn around. I got up, leaving my tray and garbage where they fell. "Hey! What is the matter with you? I had to sit through lunch all by myself. I've had a horrible day and now you just walked straight by."

She turned her head to look at me. "You deserve it."

I wasn't expecting that.

"Huh?"

Summer put a hand on her hip and flipped her light black hair over her shoulder. "How could you write that stuff last night? On your blog?"

"My blog?" My face scrunched like a wrinkled pickle.

She gave me a look that silently screamed, *really?*

I scanned through last night. G-pa's dinner, Dr. Friedman's horrible prediabetes news, battle with Mom, and the nasty attack on Alfie Adam's allergy to normal names. "Oh. That blog." I took a big breath in and looked skyward. "I was pretty mad."

I got another version of the *really* look.

"Well, you can hardly blame me. I'd just had an awful fight with my mom. The woman is blind. I'm so serious. She only sees what's on the outside. And whatever she sees she doesn't like."

Summer huffed. "Well, now I understand where you get it from."

"Get what from?"

Summer's jaw thrust forward. "Opal, you are the most judgmental person I know."

"Me?" I reeled back.

"Yes. You."

"I'm not. I'm really not," I stammered. "It's just that I was attacked last night."

Summer shook her head. "At least your mother had the decency to attack you in private. Not like you did to Alfie Adam—broadcasting your wretched opinions to the *whole world*." With that, Summer turned on her heel and left. I felt deflated and empty. I looked down at the shiny red apple. What food could possibly fill the void of friendship?

"Close your eyes. Focus only on your breath. If a thought comes into your mind, acknowledge it, but don't follow it. Go back to your breathing."

I opened my eyes to peek at G-pa. He sat next to me in baggy gray sweatpants and a T-shirt that read *Ambiguity. What happens in vagueness, stays in vagueness.* His eyes pressed closed and because he couldn't quite sit crisscross applesauce—or "Indian style" as our kindergarten teacher used to call it—his knees flopped over to the sides and his feet stuck out.

Aura, our yoga teacher, said we'd see plenty of ways a person could sit in *sukhasana.* That was a Sanskrit word —from an Indian language. But not *Indian* as in Native American. *Indian* as in the continent. Aura said we needed to grow comfortable, however it felt best.

But comfortable was a two-part problem. I needed something on my bottom half that wasn't going to make my top half spill over it. No matter what clothes I'd tried on before class, everything either squished bits of me into places that didn't have enough room or shoved the extras out openings not meant to be revealing. I needed a giant tarp. In the end, I used Dad's old sweatshirt and my flag-sized gym shorts.

I closed my eyes again and tuned into Aura's words. Her feathery voice snuck into the dark corners of my brain. I wanted to put it into a box to take home with me. I could let it slip around my bedroom as I tried to fall asleep.

"Now come onto all fours and let's do a couple of cat and cow stretches. First push your spine toward the ceiling and pull your tummy up toward your spine. Tuck your chin to your chest. Feel the spaces expand between your vertebrae. Now let your back sink and raise your chin to the sky. Take in a deep breath. And back to cat."

We did this three times until she finally said, "Sit back on your heels into child's pose. *Balasana*. Have your knees separate and let your tummy sink in between them."

My stomach went far beyond where it should. It found the floor and liked it there. I'd have a hard time convincing it to move again. And from the sound if it, everyone else liked this place too.

When I first stepped into the yoga studio with G-pa, we thought we might find people leaping about in pink leotards and ballet slippers. We made a pact before going in. "If it's filled with fruitcakes in tutus," he said, "I'm heading straight to Finnegan's Pub. You can go home. And I'm not staying if I'm greeted with love beads either. No one's putting Christmas garland from the sixties around my neck. Plus, I'm not singing any peace songs, so if there's a guy with a guitar sitting on the floor in there, I'm outta here."

But there weren't any love beads or tutus. And no one

looked at us when we came into the class, or even said hello. They all just went to a mirrored closet and pulled out a yoga mat. So G-pa and I took a gamble and did the same thing. Mine was purple and G-pa's was green with swirls on it. We unrolled them onto the floor next to a woman whose toes grew so crooked I wondered how she could stand on them. They scrunched up onto each other like they all fought for the same space. G-pa leaned over and whispered to me, "That's what comes from pointy high-heeled shoes. Never wear that crap. You might get three inches taller wearing them, but the whole time you end up sitting down because the shoes are too uncomfortable to walk in. Defeats the purpose."

I looked at my own feet. Stubby toes. Nails that needed cutting. Navy blue fluff wedged between each toe from the socks I wore to school. Mine weren't going to win any prizes either.

The man across the room from us looked a few years younger than G-pa, but his hair was dyed the color of Dad's old brown shoe polish. Well, all except for the silver part on the tippy top of his head. It looked like he'd forgotten that bit. He stretched. And made loud breathing sounds. I gawked at the volume of his breath—as if he were letting the entire room *know* he was breathing. I looked to G-pa and rolled my eyes, but we both went back to watching him breathe. I guess his stretches were the hard kind.

The yoga studio smelled a lot like the locker room on Fridays, when Coach Osgard reminded everyone to go home and wash their gym clothes. Most of the guys never remembered to do theirs, so Mondays, when the boys and girls had PE together, were a sharp reminder of how stink didn't seem to bother them much. The girls complained a lot.

Another woman, with a long, black braid and a pinched up face like a pug lapdog, placed her mat next to the old guy stretching. She unrolled her mat and then another one on top. Double soft, I suppose. She made sure the corners matched perfectly. Then she put a bottle of water at one corner and an eye mask at the other. She sat down and closed her eyes, but then opened them again and looked at her mat. She stood up and realigned the corners.

When she sat down and closed her eyes again, I counted to three before she turned around to peer at her water bottle and eye mask. They hadn't moved, but maybe they weren't arranged right the first time because she moved them an inch closer to one another. She did this three times, repositioning her yoga mat or water bottle. I wondered if we would get graded for neatness in this class. Maybe there'd be a prize.

Someone else walked in front of the neat freak. This

woman looked exactly how I felt. At least from a clothing perspective. She somehow managed to get herself into a pair of shiny, black stretchy pants, three sizes too small, and it looked like she'd also hid her pets inside too. Her whole body jiggled. I thought something might leap outside and gasp for air. Her feet pounded the squeaky floorboards while she crossed the room with her yoga mat and looked for a space.

She found one.

Right beside me.

Her stringy, iron-gray hair clung to her head with a mess of bobby pins. Wisps of it fell down across her shoulders and into her eyes, but I guess those bits didn't bother her. It seemed the hair couldn't get past the thick, black-framed glasses she wore. They looked like flying goggles and made her eyes all big and googley, like she was staring through a fish tank.

The woman held on to one edge of her mat and threw the whole thing into the air with a sharp snap, tossing it to the floor. It landed with a big puff of air beside me. It also propelled all the dust bunnies around her onto my mat.

I worked at trying to wave them off without her seeing what she'd done. She might be offended, or sorry, and I didn't want to start a conversation with her. I just couldn't look into the fishbowl gaze.

I concentrated on trying to touch my toes without any luck while the Fishbowl lowered herself to the mat. She managed to get down to her hands and knees and then tipped herself backward until she fell onto her bubble butt with a gigantic fart!

My face went hot with embarrassment—even though I hadn't done it. Except people might think I did. I glanced around at Mr. Stretchy, Pricilla Perfect, and Hannah Hammertoes. No one looked over. Wow. Grown-ups were super polite when they exercised.

Smug with the crafty nicknames for my new yoga classmates, the memory of Summer and her disgust of my snobby opinions rushed into my brain. Was she right? I swallowed, pushing the pinpricks in my stomach away, and I looked around the room instead.

Another woman came through the studio doors, but if you didn't see her with your eyes, your ears would have missed her altogether. She was thin and wispy. Her long, blond hair fell like a thin summer bedsheet down her back. She wore black, swishy pants that flared out toward her feet. Her tiny toes made no sound when she floated across the hardwood floor. The same floor that creaked with everyone else's footsteps—and creaked even with Mr. Stretchy's breathing.

She slipped a slim, tubelike bag off her shoulder, unzipped it, and pulled out a thick, chocolate-brown yoga mat. She put it down in the center of the studio floor and gave it a gentle push. It unrolled soundlessly. Perfectly. She drifted to the corner of the room where a big stereo system lived and slid a disc into the CD player. The sounds of a deep flute slithered through the room. She was the Pied Piper of yoga.

"This must be our teacher," G-pa whispered to me. "She looks like she knows what she's doing."

My eyes stuck to her every move. I watched her slip a tiny gold band around her hair, gathering the feathery strands. Her face was quiet and looked so comfortable, unlike the Fishbowl beside me, whose face had been a discarded first draft for Mr. Potato Head. My stomach needled me again. *Go away, Summer*, I thought.

The teacher lowered herself to the mat and moved a sweepy gaze over the whole room. She greeted each person with morning-glory blue eyes and a dainty, pink-lipped smile.

"Thank you for coming. For those of you who are new to our class, my name is Aura. Welcome and make yourself comfortable."

That was how the class had begun. And it made G-pa and me breathe easier knowing we weren't going to have to sing any peace songs. At least not right away.

While I crouched in my scrunched-up *child's pose* and waited for Aura's next instruction, I heard Mr. Stretchy across from us doing his heavy breathing. I didn't find this a difficult position to breathe in, but maybe he had to try extra hard.

Aura's voice filtered into my little bubble hole. "And now pull yourself gently to your knees and work your way to your feet. Keep your hands on the ground in front of you to steady yourself as you rise. Let your arms sweep out around you and reach up to the sky, falling back down into prayer position in front of your chest. *Namaste.*"

Namaste? I thought. *Prayer position?* G-pa wasn't going to like this. He hated praying.

"Praying to get rid of your troubles is like clipping your fingernails," he told me once. "You can cut them short all you want, but they'll always come back. You gotta learn how to manage them." And once I heard him tell Ollie, "Folks pat you on the back if you admit to talking to God, but the second you tell anyone God talks to you, you're guaranteed a one-way ticket to a white-padded room."

I nervously wondered if we would have to join in on a communal message to God. But it wasn't so. Aura just told us to close our eyes and find balance. "Move around from the front of your toes, the sides of your feet, and balls of your heels. Find the center."

I did as Aura told us to and swayed back and forth and from side to side. And then felt the world go topsy-turvy and a wind gush at my face. I opened my eyes to see the ground getting closer. I thought I was going to smack nose first into the hardwood floor, but suddenly Aura's hands caught my shoulders. "Steady there, honey," she whispered.

"Now reopen your eyes, take a breath in, and sweep your hands around and up to the sky. Swan dive down, moving forward to your toes, bending your knees if necessary."

If necessary? I almost snorted. It was very necessary.

"Let's skip right to downward facing dog by moving your legs back and positioning your weight between hands and feet. Feel your heels reaching for the floor."

Just then Fishbowl let another one rip. Jeez Louise! What did this woman have for lunch anyway? I *knew* everyone was looking at me. I could feel their glaring gazes. But when I snuck a peek, I saw everyone's heads busy looking at their own hands and feet. They must have been quick to glance up and spot the culprit. I know I would have been.

The rest of the class was a blur of up and downs and holding our bodies in poses with names made up by four-year-olds. There was one that sounded like you just pulled a rabbit from a hat: *tadasana*. Actually, my favorite one came at the end. It was called *savasana* or the "corpse pose." I call it *the one where we get to lay down on the floor and let everything flop where it wants to go cuz you're exhausted* pose. G-pa started snoring within ten seconds of hitting the floor. I don't think falling asleep was encouraged, but I don't think farting through every pose would get a giant thumbs-up either, and folks let that one slip.

Aura finished the class with all of us sitting up with our eyes closed again. She told us to pay attention to our breathing this week. I wanted to tell her Mr. Stretchy was way ahead of the rest of us on that one, but maybe his needed medical attention and not just personal awareness. I peeked again to see her bow to the class and say, "*Namaste*. Peace."

I liked the word. *Namaste*. I rolled it around with my tongue while copying the little bow everyone else gave back to Aura. When I looked up, people shuffled to stand from their mats. Aura came straight to G-pa and me on her fairy feet, her black pants stirring up a breeze of dust bunnies. "Welcome to you both and thank you so much for joining us today. I'm Aura, and you are?" She waited for G-pa to answer.

"Stiff, sore, and out of shape." He reached for her hand and got to his feet. "Whew! That's one workout I'd never thought to see myself doing. But I suppose these old joints will be happier for it tomorrow."

She tilted her head. "I hope you didn't overdo any of the pose positions. I always tell people to listen to the wisdom of their bodies. Yoga shouldn't hurt." She turned to me. "Did you enjoy yourself this afternoon?"

I smiled. "Uh-huh. I'm Opl. It's spelled O-P-L because I'm trying to condense myself. And this is G-pa—I mean Walter. He's not planning to come to any more classes. He's just here to make sure I'm okay. G-pa's not much for getting out of his La-Z-Boy."

G-pa's face went a little red and he coughed. "Um, well, I'm a bit past the point of buffing up for show."

Aura smiled, and I swear I saw her perky nose get dimples. "It's a good thing yoga doesn't concentrate on *buff* work then. But you'd be surprised to see how many men— and men of all ages—come to join us on a regular basis. They often fill up half my class."

I knew what G-pa was thinking, and if he had his laptop open and mine in front of me, I'd see this: *THAT'S BECAUSE THEY'RE HERE CHECKING HER OUT IN HER STRETCHY PANTS—NOT BECAUSE THEY'RE TRYING TO WORK ON TOUCHING THEIR DOGGONE TOES.* I could almost see his fingers moving to type, but he kept quiet in the mouth department.

Aura turned to me. "And, Opal, yoga isn't really something that helps folks slim down but rather *open up*. Creating space can be a wonderfully healthy thing too." She smiled at me.

"I love your name," I blurted out. "Where does it come from?"

"It's Greek. It means breath."

"Wow, your parents are awesome. They must have known what you'd be when you grew up," I said. "I'm planning to come to your classes twice a week, if that's okay."

She put a hand on my shoulder. "Opal, you are welcome whenever you can make the time. It's beneficial for people of all ages and of all types."

I wondered if she meant *you fat people*, but I pushed the thought away. I wanted to like Aura. I also wanted her to do something about Fishbowl Farter. "Do the same people come each week?"

"There are some folks who have been coming for years and others who pop in and out when it suits them. It's easy enough to practice at home."

And most people learn to pass gas at home when they're alone too, I thought to myself. I'd have to plan carefully where I placed my mat next time. I wondered if it was okay to get up and move if someone you didn't like sat next to you. Just like school. Except I was usually the reason someone got up to move.

Chapter

9

Summer still wasn't talking to me, so I had to eat lunch alone. I stopped throwing my apple away, but I didn't eat it either. I decided to give it to the soup kitchen guy. At first, I didn't say anything. I just put it on the step next to him as I walked home from school. I didn't even look at him the first couple of times, so I couldn't tell if he was happy or not.

By the fourth time, I met his eye and held out the fruit to put in his hand. He smiled. It was pretty scary. He had a chipped tooth. I wondered if he'd broken it on the apples. I finally worked up the nerve to ask him about it the next day, but the apple that came with our lunch tray turned into an orange.

The guy's eyebrows, which I first mistook for caterpillars, shot up with surprise when I handed it to him. "Hey, I ain't no charity case. I figure I owe you a good two hours' worth of work now." He pointed to his sign. "What do you want me to do?"

I looked at him. My stomach prickled. Talking to him was hard enough. Employing him was something else altogether. I wanted to run, but that seemed stupid since I'd started the whole *let's be friends* bit by giving him food. Now it felt like I had a stray dog who wanted to follow me home. Mom would be super angry. She'd told us no more pets. Especially if it turned out to be a man.

"Umm," I said, stalling. I could only think of math homework. "How are you with figuring out the lowest common denominators?" Maybe I could leave my worksheet with him and pick it up in the morning.

His face looked like I'd asked him to translate Chinese.

"Never mind," I said. "Do you know how to wash windows?"

He nodded.

"Okay then. There's a bookshop on Main Street with icky dirty ones. You can do those."

⌒

On my way home, I stopped at the public library where Mom worked. We were researching maritime trading routes in history class and were reminded three times we couldn't use Wikipedia as a source. In fact, we all had to prove we'd visited the library to hunt for real books by bringing back a sheet of paper with the librarian's signature on it!

So it did not surprise me to see Summer at a reading table doing the same thing I was about to do. The surprise was seeing her pack up as soon as she saw me coming.

"Aren't I forgiven yet?" I asked. An adult at the next table gave me a finger to the lips gesture.

Summer tilted her head and shifted the books in her arms. "In my family, people don't just *say* sorry. They make amends." With that, she turned and headed for the librarian to check out her books and get an autograph.

My heart sank a little—partially because Summer was still angry with me, but also because I wasn't entirely sure what kind of "amends" she expected.

I went to my favorite explainers, Merriam and Webster and looked up *amend*. Their first entry said, "to put right." The next said, "to change or modify for the better: improve." And then there was a little bitty part down at the end that said "to reform oneself."

Sheesh. Everybody keeps asking me to change! I slumped over the big dictionary and let my head thump on the desk. I didn't have to lift it up to know who shushed me again.

How in the world could I prove to Summer that I was "new and improved"? I drummed my fingers on the desk. Do I write Alfie Adam an apology letter on my blog?

Should I wear a chef's hat to school with his face on the front of it?

An overzealous woman lugging an armload of books and a bleary-eyed child passed my chair and whispered, "I just need one more thing in the cooking section, and then we'll go, I promise."

Poor kid, I thought. *Ugh, the cooking section.*

I sat up straight in my chair and whipped my head around to follow them. "The cooking section!"

I could almost feel the spittle coming from the grumpy reader's mouth as she shushed me for the third time. She might insist I leave, and then I'd never get the librarian's signature. But maybe I'd get something better—Summer's forgiveness.

The idea that popped into my head made me cross my fingers as I scanned the shelves of cook books. "Please be here, please be here," I said under my breath. I needed one of the Grunch's cookbooks. Any one of the fifty billion he'd written. It would probably have a title like *Say No to Yummy Food* or *How to Make a Miserable Meal*. It didn't matter which one; they would all churn out the same flavor of torture.

When my fingers landed on the spine of one of his books, I let out a huge sigh of relief and pulled it to my chest. Finally. If my words of apology weren't good enough to stomach, then I'd stomach somebody else's words instead. I decided to cook Alfie Adam's food and serve up some sorry on a platter with a little please-forgive-me parsley on the side.

⌒

At home, on my bed, I wrestled the book out of my backpack and found the Grunch's face staring back at me. His hands held a fork and spoon, perched before a bowl of spaghetti. He looked so happy. His eyes crinkled with perkiness. The name of the book was *Alfie's Meal Madness: Stand Up & Take a Seat*.

On the inside cover, someone had left a penciled note. It said, "YouTube has videos of all these recipes." I turned the page and skimmed his introduction. It babbled a lot of "The whole world grows fat and I plan to make you all healthy" nonsense. I hated the book already. I wanted to rip the pages out because they made me think of Mom's stupid skinny jeans, but then I thought about Aura and her peaceful inhalations and exhalations. She said to pay attention to our breathing this week. Mine was racing and huffy. Not good yoga breathing at all. Not too different from Mr. Stretchy's, actually. I wonder if he attended yoga class to get into skinny jeans.

I couldn't believe I had thought this would be a great way to get Summer back. Kids don't need to know how to cook. We had grown-ups for that. *They* were supposed to make all the meals. *They* were supposed to deliver the food. *I* was supposed to do nothing but eat it.

I grabbed my laptop and searched for the videos the book suggested. A long list of them came up on my screen. Each lasted around eight or nine minutes. This was a stupid idea. I shut my laptop with a crisp snap. No. No to I'm-here-to-ruin-food-for-you Alfie Adam, no to cookbooks and how-to videos, no to yoga and the Fishbowl Farter, and a big fat NO to skinny jeans.

I sighed. This also meant *no* to my best friendship in the whole world.

Why couldn't I just get what I wanted? Why was this so hard? I just wanted Summer to be my friend again. I just wanted Mom to be like she used to be. I just wanted to have my old body back. I just wanted Dad to be alive. Why couldn't everyone be like they used to be? Change sucks.

I reached over to my bedside table and opened the drawer. I took out a Kit Kat bar—something that has never changed—and then went to my blog page. I saw a new comment.

Blondiebird: Dear Opl, I saw your blog on my friend's Facebook page and clicked on it because I could really use some advice. Basically, I hate swimming. I hate pools, lakes, oceans, even puddles. I haven't taken a bath since I was five. (Showers aren't a problem.) You'd think I'd be safe, living in central New Jersey. No oceans there, right? But my mother insists that I join my school's swim team. To "face my fears" and prepare me for this grueling ordeal, she's going to make me take swimming lessons. I've tried explaining to her my very rational terror of drowning, but she just tells me I'm being unreasonable. Please help! I'm sick of my brother calling me "Aquaphobic Ariel"!

I scratched my chin and thought about poor Ariel. She didn't belong in a big pool any more than I belonged in tiny pants. We lived in a similar pickle, and I was guessing we might have been separated at birth but were still parented by the same mother.

Dear Blondie,

First of all, have no fear. No, I don't mean of water, but of being alone. According to the National Institute of

Mental Health, about 6.3 million American adults have some type of phobia. Holy mother-of-pearl! Happily, many of us ditch being afraid as we grow older—unless of course you have a fear of growing older (gerasco-phobia), in which case, you may not make it that far.

I wondered at first if you may have clithrophobia—a fear of being enclosed. How are you with hugs? Or maybe your fear wasn't one of water at all, but rather the dreaded accompaniment of most water activi-ties—the swimsuit. Do you have a fear of undressing in front of someone—like in the locker rooms? That would be a classic case of dishabiliophobia.

I myself have a hefty list of phobias. Optophobia, the fear of opening my eyes in the morning, causes me the most trouble. It usually occurs on school days.

Personally, I don't think your fear of water should worry you, unless you're totally hygrophobic, where you have a fear of moisture all together. That would be weird.

Here's my advice: according to my science book, water doesn't want to swallow you up. It wants to hold you up. Also, the pudgier you are, the more buoyant you become. So I say, face your fears with an extra scoop of Chubby Hubby tonight.

I nearly typed "Love, Opl," when I thought about Aura and my yoga class. I changed my sign off.

Namaste,

Opl

My bedroom door opened with a thump. Ollie came in with an armload of my clothes from the laundry room. Somehow he'd found my Sugar Plum fairy costume from when I was forced to take ballet in second and third grade. I danced horribly, but the instructor hadn't been the least bit picky. She'd just wanted as many bodies on stage as the fire marshal would allow and as much pink on us as a Pepto-Bismol commercial. We'd looked like the inside of a cotton candy machine with sequins.

I almost complained to Ollie that he was taking clothes from my closet without asking, but then realized he was *bringing* clothes to my closet without asking as well. Truthfully, he had saved me a trip up and down the stairs. I decided not to whine. Plus, he actually looked better in the outfit than I ever had.

I shook my head at him and sighed. "Breast cancer awareness day in first grade today?"

Ollie gave me a quizzical smile. "Nope. But Jacob

Berndowser called me a boob!" He plopped my clothes on my bed and then looked at the open cookbook picturing a big dish of spaghetti. "Are you going to cook like G-pa?"

I snorted. "Apparently, I'm going to cook like Alfie Adam."

"Who?"

I picked up the book and pointed to the cover.

Ollie tilted his head and took the book from my hands. "She's not all that pretty."

"You don't need good looks to sell a cookbook. You have to have a gimmick. Alfie Adam doesn't like happy children. *His* recipes are chock-full of ideas meant to turn your stomach and make you never want to eat again."

He pointed at another page in the book. Glasses filled with pink-and-yellow-and-purple colored liquid. "This looks yummy. Why don't you make these? They look like McDonald's shakes."

I looked down at the page. *Frozen Fruit Smoothies.* "They're pretend shakes. They won't taste anything like McDonald's."

"I'll eat it," he said with a goofy grin.

"I know you will, buddy. You'd do anything for anyone. That's why you're so squishable."

I'm not sure he heard me because he pulled my Harry Potter Sorting Hat down over his head and, although muffled by the hat, uttered something about Mom becoming a Hufflepuff.

I sighed and flopped back on the bed. "Fine. Write down the ingredients list and give it to Mom. I'll make it after school tomorrow. But just so you understand, this ain't no 'Happy Meal.'"

1 ripe banana

1 cup of frozen fruit: mango, blueberries, or strawberries

2 heaped tablespoons of vanilla yogurt

1 small handful of quick cook oats (not instant)

1 small handful of mixed nuts

1 glass of soy, almond, or low-fat milk

I looked at my ingredients. Mom had gotten everything on the list. Strawberries for the frozen fruit and low-fat milk for the liquid part. I had no idea what all the other nuts were called, but I recognized almonds on the package from the candy wrapper of an Almond Joy bar. I found our blender in the back of a cupboard and remembered the days when Dad had made us chocolate malts on the weekend. Everybody got a glass and a spoon. Mom and Dad would sit on the back porch, sipping, while Ollie and I did cartwheels on the lawn. We'd run back to them for frosty, cold breaks. The blender hadn't been used since then and looked like it had been shoved to the back on purpose. I suppose if we didn't see reminders of him, we could pretend he'd never been here.

After I manhandled the monster into the sink and cleaned the cobwebs from it, I followed the Grunch's instructions. I sliced my banana after peeling and tossed it into the blender with the strawberries and yogurt. I whizzed it up. No kidding. That's what the recipe said to do. Whiz. I added the rest bit by bit, whizzing in between, until I felt sure we'd have nothing more than pretty-colored glue in frosty, tall glasses.

I poured the goop into three cups—G-pa was going to drink this too—and watched a few lumps plop into each glass. McDonald's shakes did not plop.

Ollie helped G-pa up from his Lay-Z-Boy and handed him a glass of the pink goo. He raised it to his nose and took a whiff. "Smells good."

"Define good," I said, bringing the glass to my lips.

Before I'd had a chance to take my first sip, I saw beyond the rim of my cup that Ollie had finished his. He planted the glass on the counter with a thunk and smiled, revealing a thick, pale-pink mustache resting on his top lip. "Wow. That's just what I needed. I'm ready to go kick Jacob Berndowser's butt!"

"No you are not," G-pa announced before taking a tentative sip.

"Yeah, G-pa's right. It's hard to conjure up fear when you're facing someone dressed as Snow White. Maybe the evil queen would work better." I was growing tired of all the girlie costumes.

"No way," Ollie said. "Mom would never go for that."

"And neither do I, Ollie," G-pa added. "You're not kicking anyone's butt unless I'm there to watch." He turned to me. "I'm going with Ollie to talk to this Jacob kid's folks and find out what's going on." He wiped his mouth with a handkerchief. "Hey, this ain't bad. Even the chunky bits at the bottom are kinda tasty."

I took a sip. It was sweet. Maybe not as sweet as the strawberry shakes at McDonald's, but still sweet. And it tasted like strawberries...and bananas. And it was a little bit chewy with whatever made it chewy—even though I didn't put any gum in it. I raised my eyebrows. "Okay, so it doesn't suck. Go figure."

Ollie looked at me with his pink peach fuzz—except it was strawberry. "What will you make next?"

"Well," I said, sizing up the kitchen, "since I've made a mess, I'd bet my making days are over, don't you think G-pa?"

"Nope. From now on, when you cook, I clean. But I'll

help you with your new recipe book. We'll do it every other day. In fact, I'm looking forward to Sunday. I'm sure it'll be a heck of a lot better than any crappy chicken nuggets—or whatever Sunday's menu usually offers." He took another swig from his glass. "Yup, this is mighty nice. I wouldn't mind a few more of these now and again."

G-pa grabbed a dish towel and moved toward the sink. "You go on upstairs and finish your homework. And don't forget to jot down on your mom's shopping list all the junk you need for Sunday. She'll expect to see it there."

I trudged off to the stairs and mumbled under my breath, "Junk? Junk is a four-letter word in this house if you put it next to the word food. Junk will be ignored if it's written on *her* list."

Chapter 10

"Get comfortable and get tall. Leave your life situation trailing behind you and on the back burner while you float around and find what feels like *center* to you."

I tried picturing what getting tall would look like. I slowed down my breath, which I practiced each time I passed the soup kitchen dude. It's not that he looked *scary*; he just looked *different*. And different made my heart rattle around in my chest. But with all of Aura's mindful breathing drills, I could now manage a calm yoga wave with all the sweeping of arms practice we'd been doing in class.

I imagined leaving Mom and my diet blog, which was no longer about my diet but rather a random place people came to ask for free advice. Yesterday, a girl had written in asking, what was the best way to clean her bedroom mirror, and I had to admit I'd never done it. Since I avoided mine, I had no idea if it was dirty or clean.

"Let your *in* breath fill up the spaces inside you, and push the release of air all the way outside. Every last molecule."

We were studying air molecules in science class. Mr. Inkster explained how they behave differently in hot or cold temperatures. I knew I behaved differently in hot and cold temperatures. In fact, I had brought it up the last time I'd checked in with Dr. Friedman. We'd compared notes over one of the scary things I researched about diabetes.

I'd told her how I hated to be hot. "I read that some study showed people with diabetes ended up with broken body thermometers. It's like their internal fan goes on the fritz and they just get hotter and hotter and hotter."

Beth looked at me above her black chunky glasses, which had slid down her nose a little bit. "Are you talking about autonomic neuropathy?"

"No," I said. "I'm talking about how scary it would be if things got so bad that the only way I could cool myself down was to start panting like a dog because my sweat glands conked out."

Beth let out a funky snort but then pushed her glasses up her nose and looked at me with her serious eyes. "Opal, I want you to be careful with what you Google. There is a lot of misinformation out there on the web. But yes, you're partially correct. One of the side effects of diabetes can be damage to the nervous system, and that damage can affect how a person's body regulates temperature."

"Is that going to happen to me?"

"Not on my watch, kiddo. But remember, we're all part of a team here. You need to be doing your bit too—like your yoga classes. How are those going?"

"A little bit good. I'm getting the hang of the lingo, and I really like the teacher. Talk about one person who has total command of her climate control. Aura doesn't get too much of anything. She's one cool cucumber.

"And if I had to look like any vegetable, I think I'd probably choose that one. It fits in perfectly with how Aura wants us to think. Long and straight. I bet pretty soon it might even flatten out my pudgy parts."

"Rome wasn't built in a day, Opal." Beth smiled at me.

And neither was all this pudge, I thought to myself.

What is a knife? This was a question I posed to my blog readers an hour after the dinner where I almost lost my life. These were some of their answers:

Evilgenius: A knife is a multipurpose instrument. Made maybe as early as two and a half million years ago. It's a sharpened shard of cold, hard metal. Although one can make a knife out of other things. Especially if you've had experience. Like time in the slammer. Or a few years in the Boy Scouts.

This one was from **beautynbrains**:

My grandmother is superstitious and uses knives for all sorts of cures, good luck charms, and protection. She says that if you're a woman in labor and you put one under your bed, it'll cut your pain in half. She keeps a black-handled one under her pillow to keep away nightmares. But she says don't make the mistake of laying your dinner knife across either your spoon or your fork because you might be mistaken for a witch. A hanging will soon follow.

The last answer was from **Blackhawk**:

Don't forget all the ways people carry knives. If you're a chef, you carry it wrapped up in a roll. You can keep it in your pocket, like a twelve-year-old boy. Maybe try dangling it from your belt, like a samurai or a fancy dress military man. Or strap it to your leg and tuck it into your sock, like a burly Scotsman.

All of that babble meant nothing to me a few hours ago. What mattered a whole bunch was the piece of my thumb that joined the cucumber I was slicing for my recipe from the Grunch's cookbook. One minute it was there, and the next it was a little disc of flesh on my cutting board.

I howled like a pack of wolves at the moon. I bounced around the kitchen holding a blood-squirting digit until I'd gathered the whole family to witness my slow death. I ended up in my favorite yoga position, child's pose, holding my thumb as close to my heart as possible with the hopes that maybe some of the blood would leak back in.

G-pa lifted me up and plopped me on the counter by the sink. He ran the sting-y-est cold water he could find and put my finger under the stream. I'm pretty sure it had been mixed with some sort of acid. Then he told Ollie to get him his big tube of Super Glue. G-pa has had a lifelong love affair with two things the smartest inventors known to mankind have introduced to the world. WD-40, a fancy can of oil, takes first place. I'll never forget what it stands for because G-pa is always reminding us. It's *water displacement-40th attempt*. He says the fella who made the product was a go-getter and the name revealed he wasn't a giving-up kind of a guy. This stuff takes the squeak out of anything. And apparently, it can keep flies off cows, although I haven't had a chance to check that last one out for sure.

Super Glue wins second prize. Two guys made it by mistake, which in G-pa's mind is how the best stuff in the world gets discovered.

He loves his Super Glue and usually carries it around in his front pocket, right next to his Swiss Army knife. It gets dabbed onto everything from broken toys to shaky furniture. And according to him—and all the smart surgeons of the world—it's the best way to stick skin back together. Like the sliced off bit back onto my thumb.

"Is this the first time you've handled a knife?" G-pa asked me while gluing.

"That wasn't a knife—it was a hatchet!" I shouted. "Stupid, stupid, evil knife!" I acted snappy even for me, and by the look I got from G-pa, I could tell he held his tongue only because he knew I was in pain. And boy did it hurt. Who would have thought such a tiny piece of our body could make such a loud noise?

G-pa placed a bandage over my injury. He plopped

me back onto the floor and said, "All right then, let's do this properly."

"Do what properly?"

"Learn how to handle a knife."

"What? Dad would have kissed the tip of my thumb and given me cookie. He would have sent me off to watch TV."

"I ain't your dad," he said roughly.

"Well, he was *your* son. He must have learned his shtick from someone."

G-pa looked like I'd hit him in the stomach. He took a big breath and pointed. "Now sit here on this stool. Watch and learn. And this time you'd better pay attention."

I did. I watched G-pa clean up the mess, throw away the cucumber, and start fresh. He showed me how to keep my fingers and thumb tucked in. How the knife uses the flat part of your fingers to guide it. It looked easy. But I'd been fooled before. There must have been a trick.

"Where did you learn how to do this?"

"KP duty in the service."

"What's KP?"

"Kitchen Patrol. Everyone had to pitch in." He picked up his thumb and showed me a hollowed area on the tip. The side of his face moved up into a smirk. "I learned the hard way too."

Even though I moved slowly, and everything took twice

as long now that I'd grown knife shy, I picked up my blade and carried on helping to chop the ingredients. This was a recipe called The Chopped Salad Family. It wasn't until later that I watched the YouTube video. There stood the Grunch, chopping the same recipe. Cucumbers, avocados, lettuce, spring onions, and basil leaves—the same stuff we put in ours. G-pa and I followed his directions to hack up the whole mess on our big wooden chopping board. We even got to make the dressing right in the middle of it all.

We made a well in the center of the salad and added olive oil, red wine vinegar, mustard, and a pinch of salt and pepper. Then we mixed it up with a spoon and tossed it all on the board with our hands. Our hands! That was the shocker. It was almost as fun as working with Play-Doh, only we'd get to eat everything at the end.

When we served the salad for dinner, G-pa put a big hunk of cheddar cheese and some bread on the table too. Mom asked at least twice if we were sure we found the whole tip of my thumb. You could tell she was suspicious because she kept moving all the chopped bits back and forth on her plate. And it didn't help that Ollie kept calling it "The Chopped-Up Family Salad."

I have never had so much green food in my life, except for green M&M's, green apple Jolly Ranchers, and watermelon bubble gum. Supper was crunchy and grassy and silky and tangy and tasted like the outside world had fitted itself into our salad bowl. Dinner was a big success—not counting losing a bit of my body.

After the ten minutes of watching the child-hater whip together his *Salad Family*, and congratulating G-pa and myself for doing it right, I went to YouTube and typed in *knife skills*. Who do you think popped up right away? Yup. The Grunch. I watched his five-minute video on how to handle a blade. Chopping veg—as the Grunch liked to call it—is all about non-wobbly bits. G-pa knew as much as Alfie Adam. I guess Alfie Adam had done a lot of KP duty as well.

Chapter 11

The soup kitchen guy was nothing but a big buf-foon. And I'm not saying that to be mean, because it's actually true. Rudy "Maddog" Marshal said he'd been a rodeo clown for most of his forty-three years. He'd started off when he was twelve, watching the men who came to his father's horse farm. They bred champion barrel horses. *The best bones and hoofs in the entire Commonwealth*, his daddy used to advertise.

I found all this out when I stopped to give him my daily fruit from lunch and he asked me to "sit for a spell" so he could give me an update on the now-sparkling bookshop front windows. I knew he was going to tell me he owed me more work, but somehow we ended up talking about what he used to do.

Rudy peeled the thick rind from an orange into one long spiral. The scent of pungent citrus slithered over to where I sat, a couple feet away from him.

"There was a lot of ground training and a good bit of handling with the yearlings, but for the most part, those colts just ran with the broodmare band in the creeks and canyons of the ranch."

Rudy's accent was like slippery maple syrup—sweet and sticky and covering up a stack of homesick. He stretched out a leathery hand and offered me a segment of the orange. I shook my head. I'd brought it for him, but he insisted. "You don't know what you're missing. You gotta try it."

I took the piece from him and put the tip in my mouth, wondering how clean his hands were from sitting outside all day long on the stoop of the soup kitchen, holding that sign. I bit into the orange. Juice squirted into my eye. And it stung. But I found it easy to ignore the stinging bit because I had never tasted an orange so orangey before. There should be a better word for it. One that means juicy, tangy, sweet, and puckery. *Orange* doesn't cut it.

Rudy didn't wait for me to comment. He could see on my face how much I liked it. "A colt needs that crucial good training before it ever gets to see his first barrel. After my daddy was done with them, they moved like a long strip of licorice. All bendy round the barrels and such like." Rudy's teeth looked like they'd seen too much licorice in my opinion. The black kind that stained.

"I'd spent my whole childhood going from one show

to the next, watching the men compete and coming back with medals and trophies. Some of the competitions had bull riding—and that was what I liked most. That was real man's work. Lotta people got hurt doing that." He shook his head, remembering.

"Did you ever see anyone speared?"

"You mean gored? Yes, ma'am. Not a pretty sight. But it ain't happening often." He rubbed his scraggly beard, tilting his nose to the sky like a hound dog being scratched. "If you're gonna make it as a rodeo clown, you gotta have sure speed. And think on your feet. I liked that part. You had to learn new things to keep the bulls guessing and distracted from whatever they weren't s'posed to look at."

I heard him sigh. "Why aren't you still working as a clown?"

Rudy looked down at his foot and raised the cuff of his worn blue jeans. He was part machine. There was no foot. Something shaped like a foot fit into his shoe. Above that a series of shiny silver metal pieces gleamed. "Too slow now. I'd be skewered like a shish kebab faster than green grass goes through a goose."

I made a face. "How'd it happen?"

"That there happened three years back when I was over in Iraq. Soldiering." He took a long breath in. "It's stuff I don't much like remembering."

"How come you don't go back to your daddy's farm? Why do you sit here all day?"

Rudy's eyes went wide. "I don't sit here all the time. I work inside most every day from morning till nighttime. Washing dishes, sweeping floors, stocking the pantry shelves, taking out garbage. I help do what I can. But I know there are others who need the work just as bad and could do it just as well. I come out here to take a half hour break to advertise myself, so I can free up this job for one of the others." He gripped his sun-browned hands and twisted his knuckles. "And I can't go back to the farm. Daddy lost it all after he got sick. Course he didn't make it. The sickness got him. And the bank got the farm."

I looked at Rudy. I thought about how for months I'd raced past him on the stoop and refused to see him—just like Mom does with me. I ignored him because I was afraid of him. Afraid of a rodeo clown. I doubt Mom ignores me because she's afraid of me. It's more likely she's afraid of the big mess she'd find if she *didn't* ignore me.

"That really sucks. Sorry about your dad. And the farm."

He shrugged. "Worse things have happened to better people. I'm grateful for a meal a day here. And happier still that my hands ain't idle."

"A meal a day?" *Whoa*, I thought. I constantly grazed like a cow compared to Rudy. "Are you hungry a lot?"

"You don't get hungry when regrets fill up your belly. I think of all the stuff I should have done. Stuff that would have made my life real different, not found me on these here steps." He shook his head. "No. I'm not hungry for anything other than a second chance."

I had to go. It was time for my yoga class. I took a big breath. The kind Aura said to keep practicing. The restorative ones. I wondered if Rudy could be restored. "I'll see you tomorrow, Rudy. Good luck with the advertising."

By the time I'd gotten home, the sun had set. Aura had asked me to stick around after yoga this afternoon because she thought I might like to try some meditation. Except, I thought she said *medication* which made my eyes go super wide. I told her our school had a big slogan that always reminded us to *Say no to drugs*. After she sweetly pointed out my blunder and agreed it was a good thing to strive for a life without harmful addictions, she had me sit on the floor in front of her. She told me how we'd try tapping into the powers of the mind—not medicine. I listened to her talk about pain relief and reducing stress, but it was her *creating happy moods* phrase that caught my attention. Maybe I could learn how to tap into Mom's power of the mind. If I could find a way to help her out, she might find a way to remember how to be happy.

At first I thought Aura would reveal a secret room inside my head and give me the password to get in. Or show me how to bend spoons with my mind, which could be a super cool trick in the lunchroom. It turns out we just practiced noticing things with our eyes closed.

It's surprising what you'll discover though—even about everyday ordinary stuff—when you can't count on your eyes. Aura always started our classes that way—sitting and breathing with our eyes closed. But with meditation you might start out focusing on your breathing, but then you can move on to more interesting things. Like what's happening on the surface of your eyelids when they're shut. Mine were a kaleidoscope of colors and patterns and designs. I discovered an entire blueprint for my bedroom quilt and a moving blob that looked a little like the International Space Station.

Aura said meditation was all about self-inducing a mode of consciousness. Following that statement was my self-perfected face of confusion.

"Try to invite a specific feeling. Like healing. If there's an area of your body—or even another person's—that needs improvement toward health, imagine it as it is, then with warmth or light or energy, you envision it getting better. You see with your third eye. Your inner eye."

"Wait," I had said, "I have another eye inside me? Our science teacher has never mentioned this and we studied the human body last month. Maybe it's something you get only after puberty—like boobs or hairy armpits."

Aura had just smiled. "It's not a physical eye, Opal. It's a concept. Think of it as a space between your brows and inside your head that you can use like a gate. You find that gate, open it, and can travel to places outside of your physical body."

I stole a peek at her. "You mean *apparating*? We're going to wake up in someplace like Hogwarts?"

She'd laughed. "Nope. Not like that. I don't know anyone who can do that yet, but maybe someday. I'm trying to say you can travel to these destinations, and by that I mean a place of better health or a state of less stress, by using your mind to get you there."

This had been a lot to absorb. Finding out I had an extra eye, a whiteboard on the inside of my eyelids, and that I could use my mind like Aladdin's carpet to "go" places was a little overwhelming. Aura said I shouldn't try too hard right away. She said, "If you're going to eat an elephant, you need to take it one bite at a time."

I told her I hoped never to find myself in a position where I'd have to eat one of those, but I'd found out in the past, ketchup can make most anything taste better.

It wasn't until I stepped through the front door of our house that I remembered elephant was not on the menu tonight. Neither were chicken nuggets, and that was what I really wanted. G-pa wasn't budging on the whole *nothing from the freezer* campaign. So instead, this evening's meal was eggs. I'd spent the night before watching the Grunch make perfect omelets for himself. He ooohed and ahhhéd over his creations. It looked super easy. The Grunch said it was "dead simple." So I chose it as my next family recipe.

At first, eating breakfast for dinner surprised Mom, but I couldn't remember having eggs for breakfast. We've only ever had cereal. Cocoa Puffs, Froot Loops, and Cap'n Crunch appeared as regulars. And if we wanted a little variety we would have Pop-Tarts. Since the whole sugar thing had come up, all those were replaced with alternatives.

G-pa told Mom last week she needed to get home earlier on the nights I cooked. "If the kid goes to the trouble of doing a science experiment in the kitchen, the least we can do is be her lab rats. Make sure you're here by seven."

So with all my ingredients purchased and prepared, I scanned over the participants of tonight's attempt. I had whizzed up the eggs to a froth. Foam perched on top of the muddle mess like a kid with way too much shampoo on his head. Cheddar cheese had been shredded into a mound with only one knuckle grazed. Thank goodness it had been G-pa's and not mine because he handled injury with quiet style. I cannot pretend something does not hurt, and more often than not, I find making an extra fuss worth the effort.

We chopped a few cherry tomatoes, which disappeared every time Ollie zipped by the bowl. "Hey!" he said, grabbing another handful. "Mr. Muttonchops is a vegetablearian. He loves these guys."

Lastly, we had two little bowls filled with G-pa's mushrooms and olives. I have never liked either of these. They look similar. Both equal parts gray, green, and brown. Certainly not eye-catchy. If I saw that stuff in the fridge, it would be garbage bound within seconds. Why would anyone put muck-colored bits into their food? And G-pa told me mushrooms were considered fungus. Like this was a good thing to reveal. According to the brothers Merriam and Mr. Webster, a fungus is a parasitic, spore-producing organism that includes molds, rusts, mildews, smuts, mushrooms, and yeasts. It's a good thing G-pa didn't see me scrape off the blue fur from the cheddar cheese before handing it to him to grate. He would have told me I threw out the best part.

No matter what ingredients we used—both everyday and fancy-pantsy—these would be masterpiece omelets. Someone would have to get their sketch pad to memorialize the works of art.

After following the Grunch's directions, I had a nice hot pan with a glug of olive oil in it and my egg froth liquid ready to pour. I held my breath and tipped the bowl over until all of the yellow goop sizzled in my pan. A few seconds later, I started adding the other ingredients, layering the tomatoes, the cheese, and a couple of olives in the middle. I refused to put the shrooms in anybody's other than G-pa's for health and sanitary reasons. If he wanted to take a chance with his life by placing something in his food that the rest of us would take a wire brush and a bucket of bleach to, then that was his choice. I wanted to live until tomorrow.

The Grunch said when your eggy edges started to bubble up away from the sides of the pan, you fold it in half, cook it for thirty more seconds and then slide it off your pan and onto your plate. I'm not sure what world the Grunch cooked in, but certainly not the one with my gravity levels.

I came to find out that egg adores any pan-like surface and will cling to it like a wad of gum on one of your favorite shoes. I talked to it, pleaded with it, bribed it, and finally threatened it. It would not let go. Apparently, I do not speak Egg.

We ended up with what I called Omelet Conglomerate. No one seemed to mind that it didn't look like the picture in the cookbook because the taste knocked our socks off.

Now I know why the Grunch made all those goofy faces and sounds while eating it. Our whole table was full of them too. You couldn't help yourself. The mass of gooey cheese and tart tomatoes was unlike any of the stuff that had been coming from our freezer.

Ollie, in his Xena, Warrior Princess breastplate, licked his platter clean, as he often does, and announced, "I would like to have this every day for every meal from now on."

G-pa sat back and put his hands on his stomach, nodding. "I used to have ham and eggs for breakfast every day in the service. Kept us going all day long. They used to say, 'Ham and eggs. A day's work for a chicken. A lifetime commitment for a pig.'"

Ollie laughed so hard I thought he'd spray milk nose jets all over the table.

"I'll tell you what," G-pa said to us as Mom collected the plates. "I'll pay you each a dollar for every breakfast you have this week that doesn't come from a friggin' box."

Ollie's eyes lit up. I sagged a little thinking about no Pop-Tarts or Cocoa Puffs. Yes, technically Mom got rid of all our cereals after Dr. Friedman axed my regular breakfast beauties, and technically threw them away, replacing them with all foods beige and boring. But technically, I know which shelf Pop Diggerman stores them on for kids just like me. They go down just as well without milk in the morning when I eat them in my closet before coming down for "breakfast."

My problem is lying to G-pa. I can't do it. I've never been able to do it. He'd know in half a heartbeat if I tried.

I slumped a little further. How would I survive in school without my morning merriment? But a dollar a day would end up with a nice chunk of change to blow at Diggerman's. Except the whole sugar thing was like a weight on my shoulders and saddled around my middle.

⸻

The first morning was easy, as I just fixed the egg mess from the night before. We had leftover bits of everything— except the spores, which we *accidentally* threw away. Ollie was thrilled and went to school dressed as Astarte, the Greek goddess of fertility, in honor of breakfast. I wasn't so sure Mom would take to the idea of him using one of our best bedsheets and wearing her gold flip-flops to school, but since she'd already left for work, who was I to stop him?

The next couple of days weren't so bad because I still had the recipe and ingredients to make the super smooth-ies from the Grunch's cookbook. I even found leftover oatmeal—enough to make everyone breakfast. Thankfully, G-pa didn't catch Ollie and me making the gray goop taste

a lot better with a monumental slathering of maple surple—
that was "Dad speak" for syrup. More than halfway through
the week, I pulled our jar of Smucker's Goober PB & J
down from the pantry shelf and realized someone had
put it back empty. I went up to G-pa with the container.
"Houston? We've got a problem."

He eyed the jar with the same look you would give to a
pile of dog poo you just stepped into on your front lawn.

"This was supposed to be breakfast this morning. See?"
I held up the jar. "Not from a box."

He shook his head and shrugged.

"G-pa, the problem is there's no peanut butter in here."
I wiggled the jar again.

G-pa snorted like a hog who heard a good joke. "There
never was to begin with, girlie."

"I don't get it."

He slid his feet off of Mr. Muttonchops, who could
spot the peanut butter jar from fifty paces and was eager
to double check my findings. "Look at the back of the
label. It's full of crap you can't pronounce and isn't food
in the first place. It's a science project. Just chemicals and
pond scum."

I twisted the jar around to see the ingredients. G-pa
made his way into the kitchen. "Read it," he growled while
opening the fridge.

"Peanuts and grape juice," I shouted into the kitchen.

"Keep going."

"High fructose corn syrup, corn syrup, dextrose, vegetable mono-something-er-other—it says from palm so maybe it came from Hawaii."

"Anything else?" he asked, head still in the fridge.

"Yeah, there's pectin and salt and some sort of acid, plus two more things from our periodic table of elements that I think Mr. Inkster keeps behind the locked glass cabinets in our science room."

I walked into the kitchen with the jar just as G-pa came out of the fridge and plunked down a container of something I hadn't seen before, placing it beside my empty Goobers.

"Read this."

I picked it up, turning to look at the label. "Roasted, salted peanuts," I read aloud.

G-pa looked at me with those heavy eyes he can make when he really wants me to learn something. "All they do is smush 'em. This," he said, tapping on the cap, "is the real McCoy. Taste it."

I unscrewed the cap and dipped a finger in. I put the brown glob to my nose. It smelled like the time Dad took us all to the state fair, and I saw the big roasting peanut vendors lining the sides of the fairway. Through the white wisps of smoke and steam, a silver scoop would shoot out in front of you, a carnie ready to pour the warm peanuts into your hand to taste.

I put the goop in my mouth and closed my eyes. I traveled back in time. Back to when everything was perfect. I had one hand holding Dad's and one hand holding cotton candy. In front of me stood the Ferris wheel, whirling slowly around. Children whooped and squealed in the fun house as we walked by. Ollie slumped in a backpack over Mom's shoulders, slack jawed and sleepy from the sticky Virginia heat. It was perfect. Perfect. Perfect.

"Opal?" G-pa's hand paused on my head. "You're leaking."

I opened my eyes. Tears made everything blurry. I hadn't realized I had started to cry.

"Does it taste bad?" His voice grew so soft.

I shook my head. "It just remembers good."

Chapter

12

*A*ll throughout my class, I kept looking around at the people—Mr. Stretchy, Hannah Hammertoes, the Fishbowl. I wondered why they came to class every week. Maybe to get better. I wanted to get better. I didn't want to end up sad like Rudy, wishing I'd done things differently. At the end of the class, Aura had us all practice a silent meditation exercise for ten minutes. She said we should try to focus on our "inner-eye truth." I wasn't so sure I knew what this meant, but everyone else got down to business, so I pretended. G-pa says if you don't know what you're doing and you can't ask for help, act like someone who knows what they're doing and there's a chance you'll get lucky.

Shrugging, I figured at least I could concentrate on the truth part. I decided to list ten things I knew to be true.

1. I loved Mom, Ollie, and G-pa.
2. I missed my dad.

3. Music from the '70s was a big mistake no one will admit to.

4. I was starting to change my mind about the Grunch. Yes, he was VP for the dark side, but the dark side now served cookies. And not the kind that came in a box.

5. Cooking made me a little bit happy.

6. My blog was turning from a nightmare newsletter into more of a recipe report and chow chat. And I was super careful not to criticize in case Summer still read it.

7. The Fishbowl had baked beans for lunch.

8. I was yawning less in school, peeing less in the bathroom, and buying less at Diggerman's.

9. If you yell for eight years, seven months, and six days, you will produce enough sound energy to heat one cup of coffee. If you fart consistently for six years and nine months, you'll make enough gas to create the energy of an atomic bomb. That one I learned from Ollie.

10. Rudy needs a job.

It was kind of funny when you stopped to think about it. Rudy had a sign that said, "Will work for food" and the Grunch had been lecturing me on how "Food should work for you." It was also funny that Rudy couldn't find anyone to work for and Mom couldn't find anyone to work for her. Since Mom couldn't afford to pay anyone money for the work she needed doing, and Rudy would do just about anything for a meal, I could solve both their problems by just making a little bit extra at dinnertime and bringing it to Rudy the next day as payment for working in Mom's shop. On top of it all, I was making the Grunch's food work extra hard for me by helping to get Summer back. I think I suddenly realized what Dr. Friedman meant in her office. So much of my life revolved around hunger. I whooped with the discovery. And then realized we were all still meditating.

Polkadotsanddoodles: Dear Opl, My brother has become the most uncaring and unfeeling human being I have ever come across. Whenever my cat makes an appearance, the one I've just gotten for my birthday, he makes a point of chasing after her to scare her or kicking her if he's close enough. Then he claims it's either all in fun or an accident. I'm ready to give him a taste of his own medicine because I love her more than anything and she doesn't deserve this.

Dear Doodles,

It sounds to me like your brother feels "kicked" out of his spot. Am I right in guessing he was a decent dude prior to the pussycat? If yes, I have a solution for you. Tell him kicking kittens is a big-time crime. Smashing chickens on the other hand, is a win-win game. Not only will he lose his frustrations by whacking the heck out of these guys, but the bonus is...DINNER!

I'm not talking about taking two live chickens and making them join forces at ramming speed. I'm talking about getting deceased chickens. The kind you find in your grocery store. But don't buy all of a chicken. Just their breasts. The butcher will have kindly put them into a package of maybe two to four. At home, wash and pat dry the skinless, boneless beauties, lay them—one a piece—on top of some of plastic wrap. Now throw a little salt and pepper over each. Maybe a dash or two of herbs like marjoram or basil. Toss a fistful of shredded Parmesan cheese on top, and then lay a piece of prosciutto over it like a snug, pink blanket. Finish off by laying one more piece of plastic wrap over the whole mess.

Next, pick out the heaviest but smallest flat-bottomed pan in your cupboards, raise it above your head, and proceed with the chicken smash dance. This super-satisfying routine rocks and must have background music. Try Carl Orff's "O Fortuna." Listen to it on YouTube. You'll know why I chose it. It is the perfect cooking soundtrack.

Lastly, get yourself a frying pan and put a few glugs of olive oil in it. Heat it to medium. Plop your walloped white meat into it and watch it sizzle for about three minutes. Flip it like a burger and drool for another three minutes. Turn off heat. Slide onto plate and serve with a smile. Many will flash back at you no matter what troubles you have caused them. Everyone is friends. You can send me thank-you notes afterward. Or bank notes. Your choice.

Namaste,

Opl

I closed the lid to my laptop and chewed on my lip, remembering how good it felt to whack the bejeebies out of the chicken when G-pa and I made it a couple of days ago. In fact, it felt so good, I didn't want to stop, but we'd run out of chicken. I watched G-pa go into the pantry and rootle around for a minute. He'd come back with a five-pound sack of flour. We turned the music up higher and went to town.

I sure hope it'll work for Doodles. I feel better just thinking about it.

I couldn't sleep, wrestling with the decision I needed to make. But by the time my Nooby alarm clock buzzed—the kind that looks like an alien and has to be throttled by its neck to shut off—I'd made up my mind. I'd figured out how to handle this new employer/employee relationship. My plan was taking shape. Maybe.

I caught Mom at the front door before she left for work and told a tiny fib.

"Our teachers have assigned us to do some community service during the next month, so I thought I'd help clean up the bookshop after school a little bit each day. Okay?"

Mom blinked with surprise. "Well…I leave each day at four to work my shift at the library. That's a really nice thought, but I can't be there to supervise."

I knew she'd say this, which is why it was the only way my plan would work. "Just leave me a note with what you want done and give me the spare key. I'll be fine."

I could see mom wrestle with the idea. I bet she'd say no. I bet she wouldn't even see that I was making this huge effort to help her. I just wanted the old mom back. But I could see her fighting it. It was probably easier staying grumpy and mean. Just as I rolled my eyes and made a giant sigh, she said, "Okay."

Now I was the surprised one. "Okay?" My eyebrows popped up.

Mom nodded, searched her purse for the spare key, and then gave me a hug. "Thanks, Opal. I mean it. Thanks." She gave the top of my head a kiss and left for work.

Part one: Mom. Mission accomplished. Next up on deck: Rodeo Rudy.

At lunchtime, I thought my bad night's sleep had finally caught up with me. I swore my eyes played tricks when I saw Summer head my way toward our leafless beech tree. She slid onto the bench and gave me a shy smile. I held my breath, wondering what to say. Her lips were pressed together, almost like she'd sealed them from working. After a second, she said, "I've been reading your blog."

I couldn't hold back the massive grin that spread across

my face. I'm fairly sure it was the largest one I'd had so far this year. "I think I'm on my nineteenth amendment."

"Your what?"

I nodded, searching the sky while counting. "Yep. Nineteenth. That would have been last night."

Summer's eyes narrowed. "Sorry, you've lost me there. The nineteenth amendment is about women's suffrage. What are you on about?"

I made a small snort. "That was so true in the beginning," I said, showing her the tip of my thumb, "but things are definitely changing. I'm talking about my blog and my cooking. I chose to make amends to you by cooking my way through the Grun—I mean Alfie Adam's recipe book."

Summer's face went red, and she squished her lips together again. "I'm sorry."

"For what?"

"I guess I was a little harsh. Well…actually, Ethan told me I was unforgivably harsh."

I loved listening to Summer speak. Her words were like caramels, all chewy and sweet. Hearing her say Ethan's name, though, that made me goose-bumpy.

She went on. "He said it was all well and good to stand up for one's countryman, but more important to sit down with a friend. I wasn't there when you really needed me… so…I apologize. Can we be friends again?"

My face felt like it split in two. Ethan will definitely be my favorite husband. "You don't need to taste anything I've been cooking? Just to make sure I sprinkled in enough sorrow with my salt and pepper?"

Summer shook her head and laughed at me. And with that, it was as if we'd never argued. We went right into talking like always.

On my way home from school later, I handed Rudy a Tupperware of Smashed Chicken Parmesan and a key to the bookshop.

"You start work tonight, but nobody can know about it. It's a surprise. Let's get going."

Rudy's face smoothed out from its usual rumpled, bedcover wrinkles. His eyes went wide, the size of two old, brown pennies. "You got me some work? What will I be doing?"

I shrugged my shoulders. "Not hauling hay bales. More likely hauling heavy books."

"Books?" Rudy's face went back to extra wrinkly.

"Come on, I'll show you." I waved him on, and we walked quickly, crisscrossing the roads until we arrived on Main Street, right in front of the shabby, old store. I pointed at Mom's "Coming Soon" sign. "My mom owns this bookshop, Bound to Please. Remember you cleaned these windows? The shop is supposed to open before Christmas, but there's so much work to do, she'll never make it on her own. She needs extra help but can't afford to pay." I pointed at his sign *Will work for food.* "So, I'll pay you and you help her, except she can't find out you're working here. You have to come in after she goes home."

I told him to try the key to the front door and we walked inside. I flipped a switch, turning on the bare-bulbed lights that revealed cardboard boxes, two dented, aluminum folding chairs, and a fat mouse, blinking his tiny marble eyes at us from his perch on a bare, dusty bookshelf.

I turned to face Rudy. "I hope you like dust, cuz you and dirt are going to be best friends for a while."

He raised one of his caterpillar eyebrows. The message was, *Look at me.*

"Sorry," I said. "Just don't forget that my mom can't know about all this. Deal?"

He nodded, but then I saw his eyebrows draw together with worry. "Why can't you tell her 'bout me working?"

Because she'll take one look at you and decide dirt plus ponytail plus limp equals not-gonna-happen. I made it look like I was late for something as I slung my book bag over my shoulder and then glanced at my watch. "I told you, it's my surprise for her. You simply start cleaning up. She won't notice for a while. I'll figure out when we let her know. See you tomorrow!"

Part two: Rudy. Bull's-eye.

The next day, I told Summer about my plan for Rudy and Mom. She did not find it nearly as clever as I did. That's the bummer about having a true friend. They are not afraid to tell you things you'd rather they kept to themselves. Like your joke wasn't funny or your breath stinks; here's some gum.

Summer looked at me like I had sent Lord Voldemort into Mom's bookshop with an ax and a chain saw. "How could you do that? Think of what could happen." This was Summer's *the queen is freaking out* voice.

"You mean like the store could get cleaned, boxes could get moved, shelves could get stocked, and all at the incredible price of *free?*"

"I think it's a bad idea. You don't really know him. He could be dangerous. He's a grown-up and they're tricky. Let it be noted."

I slumped, a sack of disappointment hovering over a lunch tray with the special of the day wafting smelly fumes up my nose.

The special today was something called *kimchi*. Chef Scary Jerry, who over the past month had altered the entire cafeteria to resemble the inside of a giant human body, had taken things too far.

To get to the lunchroom, you walked through a door that has a massive set of teeth and lips painted all around it. Then you slid along a dimly lit hallway painted to resemble the inside of an esophagus. The squiggly pink and flesh-toned paint was enough to curb your hunger and have you turn back to math class. But some were the daring type and arrived into the J-shaped sack. This is the stomach/cafeteria, made stretchy looking with colossal swatches of peach and pink fabric on the ceiling.

If you're thirsty, you went to the "gastric juice" coolers. You'd find water with a blue label, water with a silver label, and milk with no label. All of the milks snowy white. No shades of strawberry pink unless you held it next to the ceiling swatches.

The pasta station, a swirly serpentine trough, mimicked your intestines. I tried to visit it often because it didn't see a lot of action. I liked it better than the salad station, which displayed Chef Patricia's stenciled quote on the wall above it: "Eat your dark, leafy greens. They contain chlorophyll—the blood of the plant." That brought us running. Yum, blood.

We had a cheese trolley, which wasn't so much a cheese trolley but a cow on wheels that mooed when rolled from one side of the room to the other. You could flip open the cow's back to reveal a marble slab in its belly and three cheeses of the day to choose from. Every day at least one of them had gone spotty with blue or green flecks by the time it rolled over to my side of the room. Summer said they're supposed to look like that. I ate the ones that were fleckless.

And I don't know how many times Mr. and Mrs. "Eat your veggies" would make us try their weekly "meatless meat." Tofurky, Better-than-Beef, Wham and soy cheese sandwiches, and Quorn are all science lab trials having run amok.

The sweets counter held nothing but fresh fruit and anything you could make with carob. It should be a crime under penalty of death to utter the words "Chocolate-less Chocolate." Our "Chef-less Chefs" painted another flourishing art display above the sweets counter. A quote by William Shakespeare: "Things sweet to taste prove in digestion sour." Now, not only do the chefs see glaring, angry children bellying up to the dessert bar, but they have hate mail coming from the English department because there has been a mass student ban on all things related to English playwrights.

Regardless, today's "Try Something New" campaign

was failing big-time. Once one person Googled *kimchi*, everyone received the copied text as fast as their wireless network could move. Kimchi is a Korean dish made of fermented vegetables. Fermented. As in gone past the sell-by date. *Merriam-Webster* says *ferment* means: a disturbed or uneasy state.

Chef Nonfatty Patty walked around with a big tray in her plastic-gloved hands trying to hand out samples. It might have gone better if she wasn't advertising her wares with the selling point, "Let's put some good bacteria in your intestines today."

The problem began after seeing the growing number of *I've just been tricked into putting my nose into a baby's diaper* faces. The problem continued with confirmation. Yes, kimchi smelled like stinky feet. In fact, most of us had no doubt it was stinky feet. But feet would be considered meat, right? So it's possible we were wrong. But still, vegetables with that odor usually got buried at the bottom of the kitchen garbage basket. Ugh.

Sadly, I forfeited my "I tried something new" sticker and passed on the stinky feet in a paper cup sample. Summer, on the other hand, asked if the tray could be left at our table since no one else wanted it, except Ethan, whose shirt was plastered with stickers. He still wrote encouraging comments on my blog. I sighed looking at him across the cafeteria, under another organ mural that said, "A balanced diet of proteins and carbohydrates will help to produce the healthy mucus your stomach needs!"

Glancing back at Summer, I saw a glow on her face that looked just like Ollie's on Christmas morning. "Opal, you have no idea what you're missing. This is brill."

"Summer, you've convinced me to change my mind about a lot during the last couple of months, but you're on your own with this gunk."

She took a giant mouthful of what looked like a cesspool of rotting cabbage, chewed, closed her eyes in blissful happiness, swallowed, and then said, "Changed your mind? About what?"

"My blog. I wanted to stop, but you convinced me to keep going. You were right. I'm enjoying it."

She grinned. "It's been a huge hit at school. Have you heard what everyone is saying?"

"What they're saying? You mean they've figured out it's me?"

Summer shook her head. "Nope. No one knows who it is, but I hear kids quoting you all the time. You're a secret success." She winked at me.

"You mean, even though my name shows up as the writer, no one suspects it's me?"

Summer rolled her eyes. "Heavens, no. There are plenty

of other Opals out there in the world. And loads of people don't even *use* their real name. You could be one of a gazillion people writing that blog. Just enjoy your invisibility. Now tell me, what else have I changed your mind about?"

Enjoy my invisibility? I was surprised to hear I finally had it. But I never expected to hear I was a success either. "I guess maybe the whole Alfie Adam bit."

She stopped mid-forkful. "You changed your mind about the *Grunch*?" She made my nickname for him sound sinister, like even if you mixed the worst parts of Voldemort and Darth Vader, you'd still not make a dent on the scale of evil.

"Kind of. Like I said yesterday, it was part of my amending plan to you. To make up for the brutal blog." Of course, I'd sooner die than tell her I'd become an addict to his cheerful, stutter-infused YouTube videos. I hadn't tattooed his name around my upper arm or anything. But I noticed certain things were changing. I wasn't hungry all of the time. Or maybe I wasn't thinking about food all of the time. But that's not necessarily true either. I thought about food. I thought about *recipes*. And how happy that food made Ollie and G-pa, and even Mom. Maybe we weren't the perfect family, but we sat together to eat now. G-pa said we had to sit for at least half an hour at the table.

When it wasn't my night to cook, I often sat on the

kitchen stool, watching or talking while G-pa did. He spent time each day going through Grandma Mae's old cookbooks—the ones he'd brought with him when he moved into our house just after Dad…you know. Most of them looked a little complicated for me. But G-pa had said, "You don't always have to follow all the written down rules when cooking. You can throw anything into a pot and chances are it'll be okay. But baking is science. You can't fool around with those ingredients because you'll come out with a hockey puck on the other side."

I also figured I should make an apology to Pop Diggerman because I was making fewer visits. Even though Mom and Dr. Friedman said I needed to cut back on my daily amount of sugar, it happened more by accident than effort. I was so busy writing back to people on my blog, going to yoga class, researching recipes, and learning about Rudy, I hadn't noticed how my candy stash remained full.

Seeing Summer's gleeful face after telling her about the Grunch gave me a spectacular idea. I knew just what Mom needed to make her bookshop Grand Opening the best anyone in this town would ever remember. And it wasn't kimchi.

Chapter 14

Dear Mr. Adam,

Congratulations! Feel free to bring out your book-keeping tally tablet and put another slash in the success column. After much resistance, you have won me over and I was a hard sell. It was like trying to convince a cat it wants to go swimming.

My name is Opl Oppenheimer and there is a very good chance you have read my blog. My friend Summer used to live in England and knows a lot of people there. From the way she talks, I'd guess maybe half the country. She's forwarded my blog on to all of them. Since England is such a tiny place, it wouldn't surprise me to find out after two or three further forwards, you'd be included in the loop. So chances are I owe you an apology. You may have seen I oftentimes refer to you as the Grunch. I'm trying not to do that as much, but it's a catchy nickname and it got stuck in my head.

My blog addresses things that interest your Average Joe thirteen-year-old. And my struggles with you during the last two months. But changing my ways was like a change of administration in the White House. It was more than just switching the paint, the carpets, the curtains, and the furniture. It was creating a whole new brain.

Change is more than a headache since I have made a routine of engraving my daily habits in stone. And ask any tombstone chiseler, they'll agree: you can't take an eraser to a whoopsie-poo at work. I like to wake up knowing what's in store. No surprises. Surprises kill people who are ill prepared for them. Or who have congenital heart disease. For me, change equals death. Well, this had been my theme up until Dr. Friedman told me if I didn't change, I'd get an effective dose of those killer surprises.

Dr. Friedman—not unlike you—was one of those people I was suspicious of at first. Although you really take the cake in that category. Literally, you took my cake. She just suggested I move around a little and eat less of it. You tried showing me my cake contained chicken and pig parts that even chicken and pigs don't wish to have as a part of them. I got your point though. And now I make my own cake. I know exactly what goes into it and there isn't a farm animal for miles around.

I figure since I have put such an investment of time and effort into doing what you've asked of me, maybe you could do something for me in return. I would like for you to be the Master of Ceremonies at my mother's new bookstore Grand Opening. She will be selling your books, so it wouldn't hurt for you to be there, blowing your own horn. Plus, there will be others attending, and many of them in my town could use a little encouragement in the diet department.

You're welcome to stay at my house, which would help with your expenses now that you have four little mouths to feed. My mom says things can get tight when your whole budget goes to the grocery store.

I have tried a good number of your recipes and, apart from one minor mishap with a chunk of my thumb, have found most of them nearly perfect. The ones that aren't, we can work on when you get here.

I don't have a specific date for the Grand Opening yet, but you can plan your visit for sometime in the middle of December. Chances are Rudy and Mom will have most things worked out by then.

I know from watching your videos that you're a fairly dressed-down kind of guy, and even though I don't think you'll need to rent a suit for the big day, it might be a nice effort if you brushed your hair.

I will wait excitedly for your reply.

Namaste,

Opl

Chapter 15

It has been four weeks since I wrote to the Grunch. In that space of time, I have cooked spaghetti and meatballs, chicken chow mein, fish pie—which tastes much better than it sounds—homemade pizzas, kebabs, and a dreadful recipe of salmon with a funky yogurt sauce (where everyone complained I must have done something wrong, because afterward it gave us the Hershey squirts for three wretched days). I also made peas and pasta, oatmeal 352 ways, and all sorts of puddings, tarts, and pies. In my opinion, tarts and pies are the same, but if you tell people you've made a tart, it sounds a heck of a lot more impressive. They are both basically crusts holding heaven in a flaky, crumbly hug.

I have attended exactly twenty-two and one half yoga classes. It would have been twenty-three except I was forced to leave after the Fishbowl stunk up the room so badly I could no longer breathe. Regardless, the distance from my toes to my fingers grows shorter. Ugly as they are, I have had to paint them a pretty color to encourage myself to touch them. Ollie suggested I put Skittles in between each of my toes.

My yoga teacher is like ChapStick for sore lips, or the laundry room iron for G-pa's starchy shirts because she smooths out our wrinkles. Even my breathing is spongy and soft.

I have meditated on tons of important issues. Like why a new section in the school cafeteria serves food made from the Good Intentions Incarnation Monastery. They make tofu (in plain, garlic, or one blessed with a healing spell), tempeh (which I read comes from fermented moldy soybeans and is then pressed into a block for easy slicing), mushroom pâté (still mushrooms, no matter how squished up you make them), and vegetarian sausage (extra chewy chorizo). I spent too much time meditating on what makes it extra chewy and ended up with an extra upset stomach. I'm still trying to figure out if the folks from the monastery are repeating their life in order to get their recipes right or are forced to eat this gunk because of something evil they did in a prior lifetime.

And during these past weeks, I have also written thank-you posts to a whole bunch of you for all of your recipes and tips on how to chop, slice, dice, peel, sauté, shred, grate, broil, bake, and garnish. If I haven't written you one, it's because I haven't cooked up your suggestion yet. I'll get to it. Except for WebMan101's Deep-Fried Frog Legs. Yeah, I like frogs too, but, dude, these guys eat flies! Anyway, I just wanted to say thanks.

I stopped typing and scrolled down to look at all the posts. I also answered a lot of questions on my blog. For instance, *How much deeper would the ocean be if sponges didn't grow in it?* And, *If there's a speed of sound and a speed of light, is there a speed of smell?* Better yet, *If a bee is allergic to pollen, what could they do for a living?* And lastly, *If you put a thousand seagulls in an airplane while it's flying, each weighing two pounds, but made them all fly inside the airplane, would the airplane weigh 2000 pounds more?* After the last one, I'd figured out Ollie was writing them.

My mind strayed further from my blog. Every day after school, I played Meals On Wheels, or maybe Food on Foot. I delivered leftovers from last night's dinner to Rudy, and he thanked me with a smile and empty Tupperware. We talked a lot about our dads and how we both wished we had them back. But today Rudy had other things on his mind.

"Is she getting suspicious?" he asked me after gobbling up the huevos rancheros I made especially for him. I had scrambled some eggs with chopped-up tomatoes, peppers, and black beans, topped them with sour cream and salsa, and then wrapped everything in a flour tortilla. The breakfast of champions and past-life rodeo clowns.

The concrete steps of the soup kitchen made a buttsicle out of my bottom. I rubbed my hands together to warm them. "You have to have your eyelids in the upright position and a functioning brain to see something and grow suspicious over it. She's not just sleepwalking; she's sleepworking."

Rudy cocked his head and squinted at me through one eye, like he was sizing up what I'd said.

"Okay, maybe a little, since she thinks I'm the one working at the store, but I guess she's just too tired to ask me much about it. She looks like a zombie when she sits down for supper." I chewed on my lip and looked at Rudy. "I feel a little guilty taking all the credit, but it won't be for long. It's December. Since the Grand Opening is a couple weeks away, she's got to start searching for someone to help out in the store soon. I don't know how many people are willing to work for a someday paycheck. I hope she'll hear our story and leap with joy right on the spot. It could happen."

Rudy gave me the same look Summer has practiced and perfected. It's the one that says, *You have idiot tattooed on your forehead.* I shook it off. "The place looks better and better. Mom loves that it's getting cleaner. And she keeps making comments about the fact that I—or rather you—find such clever ways to put stuff away. You've made all these cool nooks and crannies." I smiled and nodded at him.

Rudy shrugged. "When you're working with animals, space counts for everything. You can't have nothing on the floor they might trip up on. And no bits poking out from places they might brush up against. You damage an animal and there goes the price of a sale. Plus, they depend on you to watch out for them." He scratched under his chin. "I kinda like working in that shop. It's almost time to start unpacking all the boxes of books coming in. That's the thing I miss most 'bout the farm—all the tall tales. Late at night, after we'd finished our chores, we'd sit on the porch and swap stories. I s'pose working in a bookshop will be a bit like that. All those people with stories to tell. It'd be nice to read some of them."

"I don't mind reading stories—as long as they're happy ones. I hate books about people who are always in *bind*." I slapped my knee. "Get it? A bind?"

Rudy shook his head and sighed. "You sure do like to josh with folks, dontcha?"

I wrapped my arms across my chest and tucked my head down, squeezing away the cold. "Like to? I have to," I mumbled into the crook of my elbow. "Humor helps."

"Helps you hide, maybe."

"From what?" I looked at him from the corner of my eye, my jaw growing tight.

"I think you wear your humor like I used to wear my bright, clownin' costume. We're kinda one and the same. I used to rustle up a bunch of tomfoolery to keep a bull busy from hurting anyone. And you dress yourself up with layer after layer of wisecrackin' quips to keep life from giving you a sharp horn in the ribs. We're both just trying to distract life."

"As long as I'm laughing, I can't be crying."

Rudy clucked his tongue. "Problem is, that takes a whole lotta energy. You can't do it for long, Opal. Life won't sit down and wait for you to catch up once you've caught your breath and had a rest. Sometimes you just gotta grab the bull by the horns and deal with it."

Chapter

16

Everything moved along swimmingly except for one frustrating fact. Alfie Adam was not responding to my invitation. Correction. *Invitations*. After sending my first email to the Alfie Adams Trying to Save the World One Bite at a Time Headquarters, I waited three days. Three days that trudged on like a snail with a limp. I could have walked to England to get an answer faster. Except after the third day, I still had no answer. So…I wrote him again. And again. And four more times after that. I was officially a stalker.

In the meantime, I told everyone about the Grand Opening. I wanted a good showing for when Alfie Adam finally got my letters and wrote he was coming. Likely, someone at the office was holding on to all his mail. I bet he was making a particularly tricky section of the world healthy but they had trouble understanding his English. His language contained all sorts of words our grammar teachers would never allow. Words that aren't in any of my dictionaries and a few that most of us would get detention for saying. Hopefully, his translators translated his message with a stutter. I think it might be more effective that way because you had to pay extra attention to understand him.

But as each day passed, my frustration grew into a giant stress ball. What if he was mad at me for writing all those things about him in my blog? And this was his way of getting me back? What if he was writing about the silly, fat girl from Virginia in his own blog? What if he was telling the whole world he would make an example of how nothing good will ever happen to people who work against him—even if they've changed their mind and stopped eating fast food?

I wandered down the hall, excused from Mr. Inkster's science class to use the bathroom. I passed two of the most popular eighth grade girls, who sized me up before continuing their whispery gossip. They had such shiny hair. Unpimply skin. Clothes that had no wrinkles and made them look like miniature runway models. Teeth that revealed smiles like a flash of lightning. They were perfect thirteen-year-old female specimens our science class should be studying under a microscope. They were walking blue ribbons.

Because I was caught up thinking about how to make my next apology letter to the Grunch more apologetic, I realized I'd passed the bathroom about fifty paces ago. I turned around to trek back. When I opened the restroom door, I heard those same girls talking in their stalls.

"Have you read it yet? It was so funny," one of them said.

"I know, right? She is so totally cool. I love her snarky answers. I'm thinking of writing her for advice about how to skip class without getting caught."

The first one snorted. "She's not going to answer you. I bet *Dear Opl* gets a million questions a day. And yours is too lame."

Dear Opl? I thought. They're talking about my blog! I stood by the sink, waiting for a stall.

The toilets flushed and they both came out to fix their hair—without washing their hands!

"How do you know if she'd answer me or not? You don't write her blog," the class-skipper said, making a face at her friend.

My heart started whamming in my chest. *Could I do this?* I took a big breath and turned toward them. "Actually, *I* write her blog."

The two girls looked at one another and broke out in cackling laughter.

"OMG," one said in between fitful bursts. "You have got to be kidding me. You *wish* you wrote that blog."

The other girl threw her hair over her shoulder. "I'm so

tired of these wannabes. Especially the fat nobodies. It's truly pathetic." They opened the door and sauntered out.

My face went sticky hot. I suddenly didn't have to use the toilet. I just wanted to leave.

I stepped into the hall and saw them leaning against the wall by the lockers. They rolled their eyes at me and then suddenly attempted to make themselves look pretty. I turned to head back to class but smacked into Ethan, who was busy looking down at his phone.

"Sorry, Opal. Are you okay?" he said, putting a hand on my shoulder.

I nodded, going red with embarrassment. The girls were right. I was pathetic.

"By the way," Ethan said, "may I send your *Dear Opl* blog on to my friends in England? They would get an absolute stitch out of your writing. It's so brill."

My eyes grew wide, flying to the girls behind him at the lockers.

Ethan twisted to see what I stared at and then turned back to me, his hand covering his mouth. He pulled it away. "Sheesh! What a dolt I am. I'm really sorry. I promised Summer I wouldn't say anything and I didn't know they were there." He looked at me with puppy dog eyes. "Forgive me?"

I nodded.

He looked at the girls behind him and put a finger to his lips, then jogged on down the hall with a wave of good-bye. I glanced back at the two girls. One of them looked right at me and smoothed down her long hair. "I bet she probably paid him to say that."

Stinging, prickles of wretchedness rushed from my heart to my stomach. I wanted to run away. I wanted to hide. But just thinking that thought made Rudy jump into my head. We had both practiced hiding in order not to get hurt, and he told me that one of these days I'd just have to take the bull by the horns. I took a big breath.

"Not one penny," I said, straightening my shoulders. "Ethan would never lie. And he'd never gossip about people behind their backs. He likes me just the way I am, and he thinks I'm really funny."

One of the girls made a snort. "Isn't it amazing how the one thing fat people cling to most—apart from a fistful of food—is the belief that they're funny?"

I fumed. "You know what else is amazing? The fact that 3,895 other people believe I'm funny too. Because that's how many followers I have for my blog. And do you know what I think *they* would find the most amazing? It's that the two most popular girls in our school *still* don't wash their hands after they've had a pee in the bathroom. GROSS!"

I flew down the hall, my heart wishing it could fly

out of my chest. I went straight to the vending machine outside—the one the chefs are still campaigning to get rid of—and ordered up a super colossal king-size Hershey's bar. I walked to the old beech tree and fell in a heap on the bench beneath it. The wind whipped the dry, frizzled leaves around the base of its trunk. I didn't mind the cold. It helped numb the festering bite of their words. But it didn't help enough. I stared at the huge Hershey's bar. *Who cares?* Clearly not these stupid girls. Obviously, Alfie Adam didn't. Why should I? I wanted to be fat. I needed the protection. Fat protected people from all the pokes they got from the world. To heck with all the homemade crap; I was going back to all my real friends—Nabisco, Cadbury, Hershey's, Pringles. The only ones who knew what it takes to get through bad times. I opened the wrapper and peeled back the foil. I broke off a big chunk and held it right against my lips, daring myself to open my mouth.

An arm fell across my shoulder as someone plopped down on the bench beside me. "Opal, you're daft to consider eating out here today. I've been searching everywhere for—" Summer's words stopped short when she must have seen the tears spilling out my eyes and the chocolate smooshing into my face. She twisted me to look at her. "What's the matter? Opal, what's wrong?"

I shook my head and grunted a few words that came out

like caveman talk. Then I took one of Aura's big breaths and started again. "Nothing a colossal amount of chocolate won't fix." I tried to rein in my running nose with a big sniff.

"What?"

"It's nothing. I'll get over it."

Summer gave me her *The queen will now call out her troops if someone has messed with her subjects* look. "What 'it' must you get over?"

I sighed and hiccupped at the same time. "Bathroom gossip. About me of all people," I burbled. "Who would have thought anyone would have wanted to talk about me?"

"Who was it—and what did they say?" Summer's eyes narrowed to reveal the tiniest slice of blue.

"Thing One and Thing Two." That was everyone's nickname for the girls. "They called me a fat wannabe. And even when they found out I was writing *Dear Opl*, they still kept whispering about me. They said awful things."

Summer clicked her tongue. "It doesn't matter what anyone else says."

"Except for the *she's fat* part. That bit still kinda matters to me." I brushed the tears away with the back of my hand. It had chocolate smeared on it.

She rolled her eyes. "Believe it or not, Opal Oppenheimer,

you're not fat. Nor are you a stick like those ninnies who think that even by chewing on their fingernails they're gaining weight, but who wants a life like that?"

I took a big breath in, the frosty air crystallizing Summer's words. "They're just so perfectly put together. It feels like what they say *should* matter."

Summer rolled her eyes. "Do you remember the day I came over and you wanted to show me how to cut up an avocado? You said you always asked your mum to buy two just in case. When I asked why, you told me some things that looked perfect on the outside could turn out nasty on the inside. Isn't it the same for people?"

I pressed my lips together, thinking. It was true for the Grunch only in reverse. I hated everything about him until I got my facts straight. And I admit, I said some pretty rotten things about him in the beginning. And Rudy is no great looker, but he's the nicest, most harmless person I'd ever met. He was like a real Woody from *Toy Story*, except with chipped teeth. But I certainly didn't think that for the first couple of months I darted past him. Even poor little Ollie—the cutest kid on the planet—gets a knuckle sandwich only because somebody doesn't like the way he looks in women's clothing. Jacob Berndowser doesn't know a thing about why Ollie dresses the way he does. Okay, maybe I don't either, but

I wouldn't shove someone down because I didn't like their Tinker Bell costume. I'd have to draw the line at the Fishbowl though. Because not only does she look like she's in need of a major overhaul on the outside, there's something rotting away at her insides too. Chances are she's filled with kimchi.

"You don't think I'm fat?" If anyone was going to tell the truth about this, it would be Summer.

"No. I think you're goofy, beautiful, and funny. And I think you're starting to make sense when you talk about food. And I'm amazed at what new quirky concoctions come out of your brown bag when you spill your lunch across the table. And I think it's the hardest thing you've ever done, not stuffing your gob with junk food at all hours of the day and night." Summer took her scarf off and wrapped it around my neck. "I like the fact you've gone all crackpot swami on me with your yogurt poses and mental mind tricks. It makes you so much more interesting than Dr. Seuss's Toxic Twins."

I brightened at this. My spine grew straighter with each word my best friend said. Yes, she thought I was crazy. But she thought I was healthy crazy.

I wrapped my arms around her, giving her the biggest hug I could muster. "Summer, you're just like that newscaster, Gina Jacobs. You look in the underneath." I'd have bet anything she practiced just as many mental mind tricks as I did. Because to see as Summer did, I'm pretty sure she must have been using her third eye.

Chapter 17

We had one more day before our break for the winter holidays. Everyone at school either sang Christmas songs or talked about their upcoming vacations. Three people wore antlers on their heads and one person had a flashing Rudolf nose strapped to his face. Everything served in the cafeteria had been Winter Solstice–themed for the last week. Bowls of Mistletoe and Holly salad looked too prickly to eat. Thor's Mushroom Puff Pie, Odin's Nut Loaf with a bayberry and pinecone sauce, the Return of the Sun King Soup, and a Great Mother Caraway Cake stood untouched on a long buffet table day after day. Above the table hung newly decorated signs that said, "Bright Blessings!" and "Merry Meet!" and "Help grow the fiber of your character: eat more beans!"

It might have been easy to get swept up in the holiday frenzy, except for two things. Number one was my plan for getting Mom to hire Rudy—and that would unfold tomorrow night. Number two was the Grand Opening. The morning after number one.

I'd been nagging Mom for the last two weeks, telling her how once customers started walking through the door, she would have a hard time manning the shop by herself.

"Well, I meant to ask you about that anyway, Opal," Mom said, yawning. Her shirt was misbuttoned and she wore two different colored socks. "I figured since you had two weeks off, you could stay on. You've been doing such a stellar job. And during that time, I could put up a sign by the cash register saying I wanted to hire. Two weeks is plenty of time to find someone perfect."

But I already knew someone perfect. And he could continue to do a stellar job. "I'll bet you'll find someone sooner than you think. And by the way, I'm making a special dinner for you tomorrow night. A celebration for the bookshop opening. You're gonna love it."

Leaving school that afternoon, I ran to the soup kitchen steps for hopefully the last time. I handed Rudy a plastic container full of stuffed red peppers, my old My Little Pony hairbrush, and a bar of soap. "You're coming for your official job interview tomorrow night at my house. You might want to spruce up a bit. Maybe appear not quite so…earthy."

Rudy's eyebrows shot up. "An interview?"

"Yeah," I said, "but I consider that working too, so you'll get food for it."

I zipped off before he could renegotiate our terms and headed for home. I had to start preparing what all good cooks call *mise en place*. That means everything in its place. For instance, before you heat the pan, you chop the onions. And line up the spices beside the pot. The rest of your ingredients wait at your fingertips for the moment you need them. All the pieces floated around me: preparing my big celebration dinner, helping Rudy get a job, Mom's Grand Opening, and of course, making sure Alfie Adam would show up. Some *mises* would be easier to put *en place* than others. And although there might be fifty ways to skin a cat, I knew only one way to skin an onion.

Mom opened the bookshop front door and I heard a tiny wind chime tinkle above us. She looked around a little startled. "What was that?"

I followed the sound to the top of the door and scrambled for a reply. "Oh, that? That's just a…a thing I found in a box and put up yesterday. You know…to let you hear when someone comes in and you're not up at the cash register." I knew Rudy had to have been the one to put it up last night.

"When did you do it? It didn't make a sound last night when we left." Mom's last day working at the library was yesterday and she'd announced that she had some last minute paperwork to do at the shop while I finished a couple of odd jobs and would "keep me company." I used the time to write a list full of every reason Mom should hire Rudy.

My heart skipped a beat it could have used. I started to feel light-headed. "Well, that's because you always leave from the back door, right?"

"Oh," she said. "Right." Mom went into the back and I took off my coat and tossed it on the counter. I tried to fling my other anxieties along with it, except everywhere I looked I saw little things Rudy had done to spruce the place up. He'd made a welcome sign with old mangled silverware, spoons and forks twisted into lettered shapes. An old flour sack slumped by the front door with a word in red threaded lettering: *Books*. A hand-printed sign stapled to a stick read: *Donations for the shelter*. And the box of Christmas ornaments and garland Mom and I had brought yesterday, intending to hang this morning, had already been hung.

Mom came in from the back by her office cubby, switching on the lamps around the shop. "Opal? Who did all the decorating?" A deep crease formed between her eyebrows and her eyes darted from one piece of Christmas fluff to the next.

"We did, Mom," I lied and swallowed hard. "Don't you remember? You said you wanted the garland along the edges of the big stacks and tinsel on the counter?"

She scratched at her messed up hair and her gaze went fuzzy. "I don't. I'm not remembering this at all." She sat down on Dad's old favorite reading chair. Mom had originally put the snuggly, leather La-Z-Boy in storage because she couldn't stand seeing it in the house any longer. But now it lived in the bookshop where lots of people would get to read in it. Just like Dad. "Something's wrong with me, Opal. I'm losing my mind. There are so many things going on…my head must be playing tricks with me."

"Mom," I said, putting a hand on her shoulder. "Everyone can see how exhausted you are. You're hardly sleeping trying to get stuff ready. Just remember, you can't do it by yourself. We're all pitching in where we can, but you don't have to keep track of everything."

She shook her head, like a dog shaking water out of his ears. "Right. And I'm amazed at what you've been doing—which apparently has been a lot. A lot more than I was aware of. I guess I haven't been paying much attention, but…thank you, Opal. I just want it to be perfect." She gave me a hug and went back to her desk. I sat down in Dad's chair and counted the hours until the charade was up.

Six o'clock clicked into place on the oven timer. I had thirty minutes to finish. I peeked inside a bubbling pot and turned the flame down to a quiet burble. The scent of cinnamon escaped with the steam, floating upward to mix with the smells in the kitchen. I laughed, imagining all the aromas up there on the ceiling, like a massive odor party, each one pointing to the others from which pan they slipped out.

G-pa had helped me all afternoon. The two of us scoured cookbooks for the last week, deciding what we'd prepare. Ollie, dressed as Pippi Longstocking, wired orange braids and a stuffed monkey strapped to his shoulder, had set the table with five place settings. Confused when I handed him the plates and silverware, I explained to both Ollie and G-pa that it was good luck on the eve of a Grand Opening to set an extra plate. You never knew who would show up hungry.

Mom was due any minute because dinner started at six thirty tonight. We'd decided on an earlier time to give everyone extra sleep before the big day tomorrow.

G-pa walked back into the kitchen, freshly showered and shaven. He'd put on a blue collared shirt with a white hanky sticking out of his breast pocket. He had even changed out of his slippers. I pointed to his hanky. "What's that?"

"It's a pocket square. It's supposed to make me look fancy."

"I think it makes you look like you have a runny nose. Don't lean over too far into any of the pots."

G-pa grunted but picked up a spoon. Just then we heard the front door open and Mom yelled out. "Opal? Please come here."

I looked at G-pa and whispered, "Showtime."

I skipped into the front hall and stopped short. Rudy stood beside Mom, who had her arms crossed. He also stood in front of a husky police officer who had hold of Rudy's elbow because his hands were handcuffed behind him. The officer's other arm wrapped around a jumbo-sized box of saltine crackers.

"Uh-oh," I said as G-pa came up behind me. "Rudy? You're a little early. And I didn't know you'd bring a friend."

Rudy twisted his head a bit over his shoulder to the officer. "I told you she knew me. I ain't trying to hustle nothing."

Mom's eyes went super dark. Like the kind of dark where all the parents hurry their kids inside from playing in the yard just before the sky breaks open with crashing thunder and drenching rain. "Hey, Mom. How was work?" I said lightly. Hearing it come out that way surprised me because my stomach had relocated itself to somewhere around my kneecaps.

Her eyes went all squinty. "How was work?" Her voice

did not sound as light as mine did. "It was great until I thought I was being robbed!" Mom didn't normally shout, but when she did, it was competitive. She could be team captain at the Olympics.

"By who?" I said, ignoring the obvious. The police officer looked hopeful he could use his flashing lights and siren tonight. "Rudy?"

Mom put a hand on her hip and pointed with the other one. "How do you know this man?"

"I was kinda hoping to explain all that over the soup course. Rudy is supposed to be our dinner guest. Can we take the cuffs off him, Officer? This is not the greeting I planned."

Mom wasn't budging. "This man had a key to my bookshop! After I turned out the lights and locked the back door, I remembered I'd left a thank-you card for you on my desk. When I returned, he was coming through the front door."

"A card for me? Wow, thanks. Where is it?"

"Opal! He had a weapon in his hands!"

My eyes popped wide at this and I looked at Rudy. He swallowed and looked at the floor, mumbling something.

"What?" Mom snapped at him.

"It was a tree. A dinky little tree I was gonna set up by the cash register."

I thought Mom was going to have a seizure. "What in heaven's name are you talking about? Why would I want a tree in my *book*shop?"

Rudy and I answered at the same time. "It's Christmas."

"Season's Greetings!" Ollie walked into the front hall balancing a tray with tiny mugs of mulled cider on it. He'd also changed his costume to the White Witch from *The Chronicles of Narnia*, Dad's favorite character from the movie. "Did you guys know winter lasts for twenty-one years on Uranus? We'd be drinking mulled cider until it came out our ears." He giggled and then stopped in front of Rudy. "Can you untie him so he can have a drink?" he asked the officer. He tilted his head and continued. "Are there girl police too?"

"Opal," Mom said through clenched teeth. "How did this man get a key to my bookshop?"

I turned to Rudy. "That was a nice last touch. Chances are you would have been a shoo-in had she not seen you come in."

"Opal," G-pa growled behind me. "Answer your mother."

I sighed, slumping a little. "Rudy is my Christmas present to you, Mom. You know all that stuff that's been happening at your shop? All the decorations? The shelves being stocked? The cleaning of every floorboard, nail, and crevice? That's all been Rudy. He comes in after you go home and works through the night. You come in each morning, look around sleepily, and think I did all the work."

Mom's eyes clouded over, like the sun couldn't quite peek out to sharpen things up. "Why would you do such a thing?"

"You needed the help. And we didn't have the money. Rudy agreed to do the work for food. So I've been making extra each day to bring to him at the soup kitchen where I found him."

G-pa huffed behind me. "You found him at the soup kitchen?"

"Uh-huh. I met him almost four months ago and we got to talking. He's a super cool guy. He used to be a rodeo clown." I turned to G-pa. "And he soldiered in Iraq until he lost part of his leg. But when he got home the bank took his farm." I turned back to Mom. "I was trying to do the right thing. Trying to help two people who needed it. It was part of my community service."

Mom shook her head. "Why did you keep all this from me? Why would you not come to me from the beginning?"

"You wouldn't have hired him," I said, sighing.

"What makes you say that?" Her hand went back onto her hip.

"Because he's not…perfect."

It was like watching a balloon deflate. Just the slight

hiss without the big farting sounds. Mom's face turned the color of old fireplace ashes. She looked at the big guy in blue. "You can go now. I don't think we need you."

He narrowed his eyes and said, "Are you sure, ma'am? You want me to take him with me?"

"No, no, no," she mumbled, waving a hand through the air. "Just…un…cuff him."

The officer put down the saltines and released Rudy's hands. Rudy rubbed his wrists as the policeman left through the front door.

"Cider?" Ollie offered.

"I brought a gift," Rudy said, bending over to pick up the saltines. "I wasn't sure what to bring, so I just looked through the shelves at the pantry." He held the box out to Mom. "We had lots of these."

She swallowed and took the box, handling it as if it might explode. She looked down at the crackers and then held them out to G-pa. "Could you take…Rudy into the living room? Maybe you two could talk about army business or something. Opal? May I speak with you upstairs?"

I gave an encouraging smile to Rudy and followed Mom up to my room. She used the bathroom for a whole five minutes, but I didn't hear the toilet flush. I sat on my bed and waited, twisting my hands to calm the big hairball of fear growing in my stomach. Was she going to shout at me? Maybe she was practicing her mean face in the mirror. When she came out, her eyes were all puffy and red, like after the time we watched *March of the Penguins* where some of them didn't make it through the whole march.

We sat on the bed and she took my hands in hers. "Opal...today was surprising. I did not expect to find someone in my shop. Or find out that someone had a key. It was an even bigger surprise to discover he was an employee of mine, yet I hadn't had the chance to hire him myself." She paused and gave me the super-serious look. The one that says, *Turn the volume dial on your ears up to ten.* "And the biggest surprise was finding out the person I thought I was teaching was in fact teaching me."

"What do you mean, Mom?" This was the part where I always got blindsided. It looks like she's going soft on you and then...*whamo!* I waited and watched her eyes.

"I read in a book once that while we try to teach our children all about life, our children teach us what life is all about. I was wrong to mislead you. Those pictures of the women on the fridge. The whole skinny jeans thing. The dieting." She put her head in her hands and groaned. "Ugh. I was really caught up in other things, but that was definitely not the right way to go." Mom looked at me again. "I am so sorry."

I took a big breath. No whamo. "Does this mean no more pantry letters?" I looked at her hopefully.

"The days of my pantry posts are over. Besides, I think we've got a much better writer in the family. I'm a big fan of your blog."

My jaw dropped. "Really? You're reading it?"

"Every post. G-pa sent me the link. I love it. You tell it like it is—really speak the truth as you see it."

I suddenly deflated. "Yeah, about that. I'm really sorry for lying to you about the after-school bookshop work. But you're gonna love Rudy. He's a mess to look at sometimes, but hey, even G-pa's Christmas Stewed Fruit Compost Pile looks like something Mr. Muttonchops chucked up, but it sure tastes great. I think we just have to search for the underneath like G-pa says."

Mom smiled for the first time tonight. "It's Fruit Compote, not compost."

I gave her a hug. "Whatever you call it, it's not on the menu tonight. And speaking of, your Grand Opening Eve Celebration Dinner awaits. And Rudy too. Come on. He only gets one meal a day and I think we've made him wait long enough."

Chapter 18

I stretched out in bed, the way we do in yoga class. I touched my headboard with my fingertips and reached with my toes in a superhuman attempt to make contact with the other side of my bedroom wall. I lengthened my spine the way Aura had us practice on the mat.

She always reminded us to notice our bodies and said to make yourself aware of the sensations that speak to you. Notice pain and try to soften it. Notice no pain, and breathe thanks into those places. I put my hands across my stomach and noticed something I hadn't noticed in what felt like a hundred years. Bones. I could feel bones underneath my skin. That was a big surprise. I'd thought maybe I'd never get to feel them again.

I guess I'd started to think about food as no longer a way to help swallow my feelings. I had my blog to help me spit everything out. And my blog readers left their ideas and opinions in the comment section for me to look at afterward. I could either take them or leave them. There was no easy way to ditch a one-pound bag of Peanut M&M's once you've eaten them.

Other things needed noticing today too. Like the fact that Rudy now had a job. And that Mom's Grand Opening was in two hours. But most importantly, Alfie Adam still had not called or even written back to let me know what time he was coming. I do not like when people run things down to the wire. He might have been used to living life at fevered pitch, zipping around the world, because he had his *people* to do all the dirty work for him. But I had no people. I was just me. And just me had not heard from any of his people.

In my last email to him, I had told him he no longer had to make a Grand Speech for the Grand Opening. He just had to stand on the little podium and say welcome. Then he could smile for a few snapshots with customers—and of course Mom and me. And lastly, we could go back to our house for a cup of tea. He could even have the stinky perfumed Earl Grey kind that English people drink by the bucketful, and I could have the one Aura gave me called *Relaxed Mind*. We could then spend the rest of the afternoon correcting his recipes for us Americans. The whole metric system with their liters and grams gives me a massive headache. We'd swap all that out. Then he could publish a new version of his cookbook and I could have second billing. Or he could just put me at the top of his acknowledgment page where he lists all the important people who helped to make the book. I have written all this to him in my most recent email and yet he's leaving his plans to the last minute.

Breakfast would be leftovers from last night's food festival. I rubbed my eyes and remembered some of the best parts of it. After Mom and I came downstairs, I'd waited to introduce Rudy properly. He was telling G-pa about life as a rodeo clown, and Ollie was spread out on the floor, his White Witch costume hitched up around his waist. Bits and pieces of broken toys lay scattered about on the floor where Ollie measured Rudy's prosthetic foot. Rudy's pant leg was rolled up to his knee. When Ollie saw Mom and me come into the room, he jumped up and said, "Hey, guess what? I'm going to make Mr. Muttonchops a Transformer leg like Rudy's. He can slip his hind leg in and out of it whenever he wants."

"Ollie," I said, coming closer. "Rudy doesn't have the rest of his leg in there. That plastic bit *is* his leg."

Ollie's mouth fell open and his eyes popped wide with shock. "Really? That whole part came off?"

Rudy nodded and knocked on the hollow sounding plastic. "Yup."

"Wow," Ollie whispered. "Only part of you died."

On that cheerful note, I told Mom about Rudy's history, letting him fill in some of the interesting details while I brought the food to the table. Dinner tonight was all comfort foods. Chunky tomato soup with a chicken pot pie. G-pa and I had practiced dough rolling for days before we found a recipe that said you could make individual pot pies in small ovenproof dishes without having to worry about making any pastry. We just filled the dishes with chunks of chicken, peas, carrots and potatoes, all in a thick chicken broth and then placed a square of puff pastry right over the top of each dish. Super easy. Super delish.

Dessert was homemade chocolate chip cookies. I found Dad's old recipe on the dusty top shelf of where the cookery books live. I had to stop and think for a minute to make sure I could go through making them. Every time I thought of Dad, either my fists balled up full of anger, ready to tear something apart, or my eyes leaked like the Emerald City guard guy from *The Wizard of Oz* when he eavesdropped on Dorothy's sappy *there's no place like home* story. Neither one of those were a pleasant reaction to whipping up a batch of homespun happiness, and I refused to see myself falling apart at school anytime somebody announced we were going to have a bake sale.

I held on to the paper with his smeary handwriting. I brought it up to my nose and inhaled his memories. I couldn't let this part of him die too. I decided to go ahead and make them. It was too early to say whether I would feel any comfort from them or not.

The food was a big success and over dinner, Rudy told Mom about all the little things he'd been doing in the shop since he'd started working there. I could tell she was impressed because most of the time her mouth hung open. She said she couldn't believe all this had happened right in front of her eyes. Except I had to remind her that a lot of the time her eyes had been closed while they were happening.

Rudy told Mom about some of his ideas for the next couple of months. It turns out, Rudy's organizational skills from working on a highly efficient ranch as well as with the United States' government would be put to good use in the bookshop. And Mom said she refused to have an employee who didn't get paid. She said she'd been planning to hire someone after the bookshop got up and running, after it built up a little customer base but apparently some of Dad's life insurance money had finally been sent. She couldn't think of a better way to put that money to good use.

I met G-pa in the kitchen. He'd already heated up a bowlful of last night's chicken pot pie, but he'd cracked an egg over the top and cooked it beneath the broiler. "Great idea," I told him and started working on a copy for my own breakfast.

Clacking footsteps zipped back and forth across the ceiling above us. The kitchen was just below Mom's bedroom.

"Sounds like it's a fancy pants sort of day," G-pa grunted. "She's got her high heels on."

"Twenty minutes," Mom shouted from the top of the stairs. "We're leaving in twenty minutes!"

Ollie came around the corner with an empty bowl and a tomato-red mustache. "I smushed everything together from last night. You should try it, Opal."

I crinkled my face and took the bowl from him to put in the dishwasher. "Maybe next time, buddy. And you might want to wash your face before we go. It seems breakfast is kind of stuck there."

He cocked his head to one side. "Nah, I think it might go with my outfit today. I bet Mom will really like this one. It's my best idea yet." His best idea yet was Mrs. Clause. Covered in my old Red Riding Hood cape and the scarlet tree skirt from the Christmas boxes G-pa had brought down from the attic, he lacked only the ruffled white cap.

"What will you wear on your head?" I asked him.

"Mom said I could use her white shower cap. And G-pa gave me his old reading glasses that don't read anymore."

"Excellent." I nodded. "I hope it's well received with the crowds today. It screams festive."

He put the reading glasses on. "Not my message."

I looked at him seriously. "What *is* your message, Ollie? Is there something you're trying to tell us?"

He shook his head. "Nope. Just Mom." He left in a blur of red fur just as Mom came into the kitchen, smelling like she'd fallen into a department store perfume counter. The fumes made my eyes water.

"How do I look?" she asked, rushing for a cup of coffee to go.

"Scared," G-pa said. "Are you accepting an Academy Award or selling a couple of paperbacks today?" His chair scraped along the floor as he pushed it back under the breakfast counter.

Mom bristled like a bloated porcupine. "I'd welcome a little support this morning, Grandpa."

He slid his tattered winter coat over his arms and shoulders, flipping back the frayed corduroy collar. "Pfft. You've got my support. But I won't act like your paparazzi and rile up your nerves further. Aren't you just going to flip the front door sign from *closed* to *open*?"

"No," I jumped in as Mom began to answer. "There's a little podium where the Grand Master of Ceremonies will make a speech just before we do the ribbon cutting ceremony and let people pass through the doors."

Both Mom and G-pa turned to look at me.

"Grand Master of Ceremonies?" Mom repeated. "I didn't ask anyone—"

"But I did. It's part of my Christmas present surprise for you and the shop. Just wait." I swallowed nervously. "It'll be a good speech."

"I'm bringing my paper," G-pa announced, heading for the front door. "I'll see you all in the car."

When we swung past the store front on Main Street and into a parking space across the road, we saw Rudy already at work. The podium stood off to the side so it wouldn't block the view of the shop's entrance. The big sign *Bound to Please Bookshop* covered in gold garland hung above the front door. A braid of shiny gold rope with tassels on the ends surrounded the door itself. Two whittled wooden posts stood in front of the door, sunk into five-gallon Crisco drums filled with sand. A red-and-white ribbon looped across the posts. Actually, it was a homemade streamer made from old Campbell tomato soup labels taped together. Rudy sure knew the meaning of thrifty and salvaged a lot from the soup kitchen. I flashed him a big thumbs up as I crossed the street.

Mom rushed up behind me and spluttered. "Rudy, it's fabulous. Thank you, thank you, thank you!"

Basically, everything was ready for the Grand Opening. The display counters showcased the latest novels. The children's section had a beanbag chair and some colorful mats on the floor. Dad's old comfy chair would be an enticing invitation once G-pa left it. And soft holiday music played over the speaker system. Mom even had a pot of mulled cider with little paper cups on a table by the entrance right next to a plate of gingerbread men I made two days ago.

A couple of people started to gather outside on the sidewalk, peeking in through the frosted-glass windows. Mom had let Ollie do the windows. Spraying white paint all around the edges and corners was enough to inspire his imagination, but Mom stopped him before he could cover the hardwood floors in fake snow.

I set out napkins at the treats table and started taking inventory of the people I'd invited who'd showed up already. Summer and Ethan waved to me through the glass. I waved back. I hoped Summer wasn't paying too much attention because I waved a little bit longer to Ethan than to her.

Beth Friedman stood behind them, her scrubs peeking from beneath her winter coat. Chefs Jerry and Patricia had called Mom last week to ask if they could set up a table outside with samples of the new menu line they were serving in school. Apparently, it went along with their new book, which Mom said she'd stock in the store. I don't know if they'd find much success. *Bottoms Up! A Guide to the Healthiest Colon Ever* had not inspired a lot of interest at school—that was for sure.

In the back of the gathering crowd I saw my yoga posse. A head of white-gold hair and sparkling eyes belonged either to Aura or our Main Street's Christmas tree angel. Maybe the angel had popped off her spire and floated down to the bookshop for a look. Mr. Stretchy was not stretching. But I did see a larger cloud of air crystals above his head than anyone else's. I guess he was still yoga breathing.

Hannah Hammertoes stood beside the Fishbowl. Her lips had the look of a drawstring purse. And instead of blinking, her eyes pinched shut as if she was squeezing something out. I figured either the Fishbowl was passing a load of cheek squeakers or Hannah wore her toe-crushing shoes. Regardless, it was good of them to come and I was happy the twenty flyers I'd taped to the entrance of the yoga studio and the thirty I'd rolled up inside each yoga mat had gotten got the message out.

I recognized a few more people from school. Mr. Inkster had just driven by in his hydrogen car with a bumper sticker that said, "Obey Gravity. It's the Law!" And even Principal Souresik walked toward us. He must have read my school flyers too. They were kind of hard to miss. If he hadn't caught sight of one of the seventy-five I'd pasted up around school, then surely he'd taken the time to read one of the ten I'd plastered across the windshield of his car.

Ollie peeked out from behind me. "Double darn!" he said, scrunching up his face and stamping his little black boot. "The Bulldozer is here."

"Who's that?" I turned from the window to look at him.

"Jacob Berndowser. The big turd."

"Is this the guy who's been giving you trouble at school? The one who keeps pushing you down?"

Ollie nodded.

"Have you told Mom about him?"

He shrugged. "Sort of. She talked to my teacher, but the whole thing's kinda about Mom."

"I thought it was about…your costumes." Everyone at home was trying to be patient with Ollie's dress-up phase, but I guess the Bulldozer wasn't the tolerant type.

He shrugged again. "That too." He took a big breath and put his hand on the doorknob. "Well, I'm not going to let him ruin Mom's day. I'm sick of him pushing me around."

"Attaboy," I said a little uncertainly. I wasn't so sure Mrs. Clause gave off the impression of someone not to be messed with, but I applauded his attitude.

And in thinking about attitudes, mine began to sink. Cranking my head to see up and down the street, I could make out no fancy cars, no limousines, no police escort. Where in the world was my Grand Master of Ceremonies? How could this be a Grand Opening with no Grand Opener?

I looked at the clock. We had five minutes till speech time. A knock on the window startled me. I turned to see the postman, holding up a stack of mail and his eyebrows in question. I opened the door to let him in.

"Congratulations on the big day," he said, handing me the stack. "A couple of things were piling up at the post office for the bookshop. I figured your mom has been too busy to pick them up. So I thought I'd drop them off. I hope to stop in later and have a browse around, okay?"

"Sure," I said, slumping a little. *Looks like you're not going to miss anything sticking around right now.*

I tossed the mail onto the counter, but it scattered to the floor behind the register. Mom might bristle if she stepped on all of that when she came to ring up the first customer. I went round the other side to pick everything up. Kneeling on the floor, I found a couple of trade magazines from publishers with their new book lists, a bill from the electric company, a postcard from my great-aunt Gladys, congratulating Mom on the new shop, and a big envelope with my name on it, but the bookshop's address. The postmark said, "London, UK."

I felt my mouth go dry. My hands felt like the pasty, thick dough G-pa and I kept trying to work with to make pie crusts. I fumbled with the flap, sliding a finger beneath the sticky seal, and pulled back sharply when the zing of a paper cut zigzagged through me. I hissed and then sucked on the stinging part. After a couple of seconds I used my shoe to hold down the edge of the flap, tearing it open.

I looked up at the clock. Three minutes till showtime. I didn't really want to see this, I kept telling my shaking hands as they reached inside the envelope. They pulled out a large, glossy photo of Alfie's goofy smiling face. He wore his chef clothes. All white. It looked like he'd scrawled his first name across the bottom of the picture with a big X underneath it. At least I think it was his first name. Maybe he'd had Maya Papaya write it.

A paper clip held a note attached to the photo. It read,

Dear Opl,

First of all, congrats on such a stellar job with your learning to cook. I'm sure you're an inspiration to all thirteen-year-olds out there who are now taking those first steps to follow your lead. Keep up the great work!

I'm sorry my schedule doesn't allow for traveling to your mum's new bookshop opening, but it was incredible of you to think of me. Tell her cheers from me. I hope her cooking section proves hefty enough to hold all my books and the many out there that

*encourage folks to eat well and wisely. Hey, maybe
you'll have a book in that section one of these days!*

*Thanks for your support in Meal Madness and
keep spreading the word. Have a brilliant Grand
Opening.*

Cheers,

Alfie

The old me would have crushed the letter between my
hands. I would have made my fists into car crunching, com-
pact smashing, lethal weapons and then pounded the letter
into the rubber matting beneath the cash register. But parts of
the old me were still here. The parts that gave in to the rush of
hot emotions, feeling the accompanying stinging tears streak
down my face. I didn't want to care. But I could imagine that
both Dr. Friedman and Aura would have told me that the
caring part of me was not a part I should skinny up. But I still
wanted to send Alfie Adam's words to someplace I wouldn't
have to see or hear. "He's not coming." I kept saying it over
and over again and hugged myself tight with the words.

I felt a hand draw me up by the shoulder. Two big hands
pull me into a soft, flannel-shirt hug. G-pa stroked my hair
and rubbed my back. "What is it, Opal?"

"He's not coming. He was never coming. I'm stupid for believing in him. I'm stupid for trusting that anyone is going to be there when I need them. And I'm ugly and I'm fat."

G-pa pushed me back so he could see my face. It was soggy and splotchy red. I could see it reflected in the pint-sized shiny safe Mom had installed beneath the cash register.

"Number one, girlie, you are not stupid. You are never stupid for having faith in a person you care about." He pointed to Alfie's headshot beside me. "I take it you invited Mr. Adam to the shop's first day, like you invited half the town it seems. If he isn't coming, it's because he can't, not because he won't. There's a difference."

I grunted.

"This guy taught you a lot, Opal. But just because he isn't here doesn't mean you have to throw it all away."

"What's the point?" I ran a sleeve under my nose.

"The point is," G-pa said, pulling his handkerchief from his pocket and getting back onto his feet, pulling me up with him, "he was a good teacher. But he has a lot of people to teach. And the guy has found how to do it in a big, broad way. It would take too long one-on-one."

I blew into G-pa's hanky. I thought about sending it back to England with Alfie's picture.

"And another thing," G-pa said. "You're not fat and

you're not ugly." He squeezed me back into a rough, smushy hug. "That's something else we can thank that fellow for."

"Not making me ugly?"

"Nope. Ugly's on the inside. I think what you did for your ma and this guy Rudy is a beautiful thing. Ugly people are full of hate and selfishness—and don't forgive. You might have gotten the goofy-looking gene from me, but that's not ugly. Goofy you can fix with mascara or hair gel or something. It's that we're in the kitchen together. We're talking about food and old recipes. We're making new ones. You're feeding people you love. That's top-notch stuff. That guy Adam had a lot to do with it."

"You did too, G-pa." I squeezed him back.

"Let's not give up though. Just cuz the guy can't make it to your party, doesn't mean you should cancel the party, okay? We gotta keep cooking good stuff."

The party. I swallowed hard. Who's going to give the speech? I had it all planned out. I looked up and wiped my eyes again. "G-pa? Alfie Adam was supposed to give a dedication speech. I don't have anyone now."

"Sure you do. How 'bout his second in command? The person who has studied him for these last few months?"

I pulled back. "Me?" I shook my head. "I can't do it. I wouldn't know what to say."

He put an arm around my shoulder and walked me

toward the door. "It's like cooking a new recipe. Sometimes you just have to trust the right stuff will come out. Have a little faith in *yourself*, Opal."

We put our coats on. G-pa opened the door and we stepped out into the silvery, crisp morning. People rubbed their hands together and stomped their feet to stay warm. I looked back and saw Mom peeking out the window, nibbling on her nails. I ran back in and pulled her outside to stand next to Rudy at Chefs Jerry and Patricia's table. They were handing out samples of their Beautiful Bowel Beverage line. I think it should be renamed The Super Duper Pooper Scooper. It didn't sell well at school.

I tapped Mom on the shoulder. "Mom? My surprise can't make it, so I'm filling in last minute. Are you okay with that?"

Mom turned to look at me and her face broke out into a sunny smile. "You're going to officially open the store? At the podium?" She looked out at the gathering crowd.

I nodded, feeling my stomach bunch up in knots. G-pa winked at me from behind Mom. "Uh-huh. Should I go up there—" Someone shouted in the crowd and people spread apart like the circled waves of water when you throw a pebble into a pool.

"I AM NOT!" we all heard Ollie shout.

"YOU ARE TOO. YOU'RE A BIG OL' PANSY GIRL!"

That was Jacob Berndowser a split second before Ollie took a running leap and head-butted him in the stomach. The Bulldozer got dozed. A collective gasp came from everyone around them as they wrestled on the ground, little fists snatching at one another, little legs tangled up in our Christmas tree skirt. Ollie lost his shower cap.

I saw Mom rush toward them, the crowd splitting like she was Moses leading the way through the Red Sea. "Ollie!" she shouted. But before she reached them, a gold tasseled circle flew through the air and lassoed around the boys, pulling them to a standstill. Or a laystill.

Everyone turned to look at where it came from. Rudy held the other end of the rope. He'd ripped it off the entrance. I guess it doesn't take two feet to make a good cowboy.

Wow, I mouthed at him. He followed the rope to where the two boys lay and I scurried after him with G-pa behind me.

"What in the world?" Mom said, pulling the boys up and unlooping them. My Red Riding Hood cape had a gaping rip down the back, our tree skirt may have been capable of hiding the ugly plastic Christmas tree stand, but it couldn't cover up the holes in Ollie's favorite pants. The last pair of pants Dad bought him before he left and were now way too tight to be comfortable. Tears spilled from his eyes, snot leaked from his nose. He cried harder than I'd ever seen him cry. Boy, this Bulldozer kid must really be mean.

But Jacob Berndowser whimpered too. Maybe because of the bloody nose Ollie gave him. *Way to go, buddy!* I thought. Mr. Berndowser leaped over about three shoulders' worth of people. He scooped up Jacob with one hand, clamping a handkerchief down on his son's bloody nose.

"Aw jeez, I'm so sorry," Mr. Berndowser kept saying over and over again to Mom. "What happened? I was working on my Blackberry and when I looked up our guys were going at it with left hooks and uppercuts."

"He's a big ol' pansy, wearing girlie clothes, Dad," Jacob shouted. He sounded like Elmer Fudd with his nose held shut.

"Jacob!" Mr. Berndowser's eyes went wide. He turned to Mom. "I'm really sorry. We've already talked about this at home. Jacob's having such a hard time since I got divorced. Lashing out at everything."

"I'm not a pansy." Ollie reeled back, his little hands clenched into fists. "I'm trying to give my mom ideas!"

Mom grabbed Ollie by the shoulders and gently turned him toward her. "Give me ideas? For what?"

"So that Dad will come back!" His eyes still sparkled with fresh tears. And within seconds, so did Mom's.

She blinked several times, trying to keep everything inside and swallowed. "He's not coming back, Ollie."

"But he might if you just tried some of my ideas!"

Mom frowned. "What are you talking about?"

"I heard Dad say it! On that last day. He said that it made him *sick* that you weren't the person you were meant to be. That there was a lot of stuff you had to do. That you had to go find out who you could become. And since Dad left I've been trying to help you. All these costumes are my ideas. Maybe Dad wanted you to be a nurse or a flashy pop star and then he could come back. Why won't you even try?" he demanded. His face wrinkled with pain, with almost two years of misunderstood efforts.

Now Mom's face couldn't hold back. No matter how many times she tried to blink, she couldn't keep the tears from leaking out. "Honey, I have been trying." She pointed back at the bookshop. "I didn't realize what you were doing for me. I'll probably never be a nurse, and I'll definitely never be a pop star, but I'm trying to be a bookshop owner. I think that's an honest effort, yes?"

"So why wouldn't he come back?"

Mom took a big breath in and looked upward. She shook her head. "Because people who die *can't* come back. It doesn't…work that way."

"Even if he saw you trying to be what he wanted?"

Mom nodded. "Ollie, when I found out Daddy was very sick, I wanted to go with him. But he convinced me I had a lot left to do. That I hadn't finished my own living yet. It's been hard—for all of us, but I'm trying to find out what *I* want to do. That's what he really wanted. Does that make sense?"

Ollie stared blankly into Mom's face. "He can't come back?"

"Nope," Mom said sadly. "But he's here in a different way. I see him everywhere. In you and Opal…and G-pa. He's around." She scooped up Ollie in her arms, sniffled into his shoulder, and then turned to smile at me. "We'd better get this show on the road, okay?"

I snuffled back my own tears and felt G-pa's hands on my shoulders from behind. He kissed the top of my head. "Go gettum, tiger."

I walked to the podium and stepped up on the rickety platform. I cleared my throat and looked across the crowd. My tongue felt like a giant rubber wedge, which was fine because I couldn't think of anything to say. How different could this be from writing a blog? When I sat on my bed and cracked open my laptop, the words just poured out. So I put my hands on the podium surface and closed my eyes, pretending to type.

"Last week, I had to write a report for English class.

I chose the book *To Kill a Mockingbird* by Harper Lee. I picked this quote to write about: 'You never really understand a person until you consider things from his point of view—until you climb inside of his skin and walk around in it.'" I paused here and opened my eyes. My heartbeat thumped loudly in my chest. I didn't really want to say this next part, but it spilled out anyway.

"I wrote about this because it described everything I wanted people to know about me. That I felt judged. And when I finished my report, I realized something else. I judged other people." I looked at all the eyes in the audience and wondered if anyone was going to jump up and point at me with an, *I knew it!*

"I suppose books are a lot like people. It's easy to judge its outside. Or *mis*judge it. It's super easy to say we don't like its color or the size is all wrong. The print is too small. Its pages too thin. But then, if you can see past all of that...I mean...past what bothers you, you climb inside its skin. You open the cover. Someone's insides speak to you. And I don't mean that in any gross way."

I took a second to look at Rudy and hoped he could see me grabbing my bull by the horns. "In here, you see everything from their eyes and not your own. You smell and hear and taste and feel from the inside of them. The person you spent the past few minutes looking for reasons not to like.

"If you're patient, and sometimes you have to be super patient…you'll see the color you didn't like before isn't as awful as you once thought. Maybe you'll find out that what they eat for lunch isn't so weird, and it only looked weird but tasted wonderful. You might find that what they say out loud is exactly what you've wanted to say, but only ever wrote about in your diary.

"The stuff they see and tell you about is stuff you didn't know before. Or hadn't thought about that way. Or maybe you had but felt alone in thinking it. Sometimes, hearing a person say out loud the words that have been silently floating around in your head…erases the doubts that clogged up your mind."

I looked back at the door Rudy decorated and then over at the crowd again. I pointed behind me. "I think walking into a bookshop is like walking into a party—one filled with people you've never met, but who are dying to meet you. They only want you to like them. They're not going to judge you…like you do them."

Ethan winked at me from where he and Summer stood in the back. I met Mom's eyes.

"I'm so excited my mom has decided to open this bookshop here in town, and that basically, she's arranged a party you can join anytime you want to. I hope you'll come to it. I hope you'll make some new friends." I glanced around at the crowd one last time and smiled. "I hope you'll learn to be an open book. All your insides are what truly matters. That's where the stories wait. In the underneath."

Everyone was silent. Their cheeks and noses red from the cold. Their breath hovering above them. White word bubbles with no words. Someone started to clap. I turned to see Rudy, smiling just enough to show a chipped tooth, his hands coming together strong and loud. Everybody else joined in.

Heat prickled the frozen parts of my face. Mom came rushing toward me, Ollie in tow. Her face had fresh tears on it, but I'm pretty sure she wasn't faking her smile. She gave me a massive hug.

"I'm so proud of you, Opal. Dad would be bursting at the seams." She squeezed me harder. "Thank you for everything. For all your help, for all your surprises, and for helping me see things through your eyes. You are such a beautiful gem—inside and out. It's why we named you Opal. Its definition is exactly you."

"The definition of an opal?" I asked. I thought of the common, worthless potch.

Mom nodded. "It's from the Greek word *opillos*."

I pulled back to look at her. "I was named after a Greek word?" *Like Aura? The goddess of all things bright and beautiful?*

"Yup. Didn't we ever tell you?"

"No. What does it mean?"

"All seeing." She wiped her eyes. "It's true. You have a special gift for seeing things in an extraordinary way… Just like you said, in the underneath." She kissed my forehead, grabbed my hand, and motioned to the crowd. "Come on. Let's get this party started."

Jollyolly: Dear Opl, Did you ever notice that if you blow in Mr. Muttonchops's face, he gets mad, but when you take him on a car ride, he sticks his head straight out the window?

Opl: GO TO BED, OLLIE!

Dear Opl's Resource Page

GET UP, GET GOING, GET HEALTHY!

D o you want to learn to cook like Opal? Or maybe you want to keep your body healthy and strong. Join Opal and embrace food for your lifestyle. Here are some great places providing the tips and tricks you need, including fun recipes, family resources, organizations and more.

For Kids:

Jamie Oliver

jamieoliverfoodfoundation.org

(Many of Opl's recipes were inspired by YouTube videos from Jamie's Ministry of Food!)

Let's Move!

America's Move to Raise a Healthier Generation of Kids

letsmove.gov

We Can!

Ways to Enhance Children's Activity and Nutrition

nhlbi.nih.gov/health/educational/wecan/

Chop Chop

ChopChopKids is an innovative nonprofit organization whose mission is to inspire and teach kids to cook real food with their families.

chopchopmag.org

Ingredient

The magazine for kids curious about food.

ingredientmag.com

For Teachers & Educators:

FoodCorps

A nationwide team of AmeriCorps leaders who connect kids to real food and help them grow up healthy.

foodcorps.org

The Edible Schoolyard Project

The Edible Schoolyard Network connects educators around the world to build and a share a K–12 edible education.

edibleschoolyard.org

Food Play Productions

Turn kids on to healthy habits with national award-winning theater shows.

foodplay.com

Teen Truth Film Series (specifically Body Image)
teentruth.net

For Parents:

Parent Further

A Search Institute resource for families.

parentfurther.com

Joslin Diabetes Center

The world's largest diabetes research center, diabetes clinic, and provider of diabetes education.

joslin.org

American Diabetes Association

diabetes.org

National Eating Disorder Association

nationaleatingdisorders.org

1-800-931-2237

Stop Obesity Alliance

Talking to your children about weigh and health.

stopobesityalliance.org/blog

Center on Media and Child Health

Nurturing Children's Health & Development in Media-Rich Environmentscmch.tv

Acknowledgments

My heartfelt gratitude to: Jennifer Unter—it's a privilege to call you my agent—Steve Geck, editor extraordinaire; and the ingenious team that is Sourcebooks. A huge thank you to Abby Murphy, whose sharp eyes and kind words were the first to nudge this story into place. One to Han Nolan for taking the time to dish out encouragement and valuable guidance. And one to Emma Dryden too—the editorial fairy godmother every tale desires. I owe a score of profound thank yous to Rhea—my personal Aura. Lastly, massive hugs to Gabe for asking all the questions and to Chloe for providing all the answers.

About the Author

Shelley Sackier is an author and blogger who writes about the everyday ordinary grand slams and gruesome snafus in completing the Herculean task of raising two healthy human beings. Ultimately she hopes to impart the necessary knowledge of how to balance their checkbooks and pay their taxes. Her greatest hope is to discover that parallel universes are a reality, and that somewhere she is living a life where her children have agreed to occasionally make eye contact with her. They live in the Blue Ridge Mountains of Virginia.

You can read more of her work, illustrated by Robin Gott, at peakperspective.com.